THE MURDER IN THE PRECINCT

Book Two

Clara Young Series

RENEE
MARSKI

ISBN: **9781708345129**

Table of Contents

ACKNOWLEDGEMENTS

First, I would like to thank all my readers who supported me and got me to this point. I can't believe that here I am with a second Clara book. The outpouring of love and support for the first book really made the second one possible.

Next, I'd like to thank my Grandpa Barnes. His love of mysteries inspired me to read them when I was younger. His excitement to receive each new book really makes this all worth it.

For Kadee Lark and Dana Linn, you ladies are the real MVPs. It's with your support and encouragement that we are here again with another Clara book.

My husband, for making sure I have the best equipment I needed to be able to continue on this writing journey. Thanks for being my ride or die, babe.

1.

SOMETHING IS AFOOT

Clara glanced around the apartment for the fourth time, trying to think of something she could do. She had already cleaned the kitchen, vacuumed, and made the bed. With the place being so small, there really wasn't a whole lot in the way of cleaning. She tapped her fingers on the olive green counter while looking at the clock on the wall – a basic white-faced clock that you could buy for cheap at any store. Anthony had classes all day, then waited on tables in the evening at the local diner. Clara had all day to herself with no idea what to do.

They had discussed whether or not she should get a job. The issue was that once she started school in the spring, she would have to quit. Anthony didn't think it was worth it. He suggested

1

that Clara just relax until she started school. The only issue with that was ... Clara didn't take to relaxing very well. She liked to be doing things, handling things. She sat down at the kitchen table and pulled her laptop toward her. As she did, she brushed her freshly cut bangs out of her face. Maybe she could find something interesting on the internet.

She started with general searches about the town, looking for information about its history. Being a Texas coast town, it had a lot more history than anywhere else she had ever lived. And more hurricanes. From what Clara could easily find online, the community had been established in the early 1800s as a mining town. After the state capital had been established nearby, the college had sprung up, which had given the community its reputation as a "college town." Typical small-town stuff. Clara decided to dig deeper, see if the town had any dirty secrets she could scrounge up. She did see that the sheriff's "solve rate" for local crimes was 72%, which was very good. Expanding upon that, she discovered something odd. Murder wasn't a frequent occurrence, but the one murder that had happened in the last 10 years had never been solved. Even stranger was the fact that it had happened in the precinct, of all places.

Her curiosity sparked, Clara began pulling up old news articles about the murder. She learned that an intern at the precinct, a college student, had been found in the evidence locker, stabbed to death. The knife had never been recovered. The precinct was old, so the security system at the time hadn't been updated with any of the latest tech. It had cameras, but there was a blind spot, right where the intern had been discovered. This meant that someone knew about that blind spot. Clara decided to dig deeper into the intern's past, maybe figure out what could've triggered the murder.

The victim, Kelly Jo Howard, was a local girl who had grown up right there in town. She had graduated at the top of her class and been accepted by many colleges, but had decided to attend the one closest to home so that she could help her mother take care of her younger sisters. Kelly Jo had interned at the precinct three days a week, then worked at the diner the other four days. She had decided to major in criminal justice and she had been using the internship to learn everything she could about the police force. Clara stared at the picture she had found online. The girl had been Clara's age, with curly black hair, dark skin, dark eyes, and dimpled cheeks. There was so much promise in those clear eyes, so much hope. Snuffed out for a reason no one could seem to decipher.

Next, Clara started looking into the internship. That was something she could do this fall while waiting for the spring semester. She had already decided to go the criminal justice route, much to her mother's frustration. Going into law enforcement just felt natural. From what Clara could tell, the precinct didn't normally offer internships during the fall or spring, only summer, but she had a feeling they would make an exception for her. She pulled out her phone and gave her dad a quick call.

"Hey sweetie," he said. "How's it going out in Texas?"

Clara sat back, enjoying the sound of his voice. "It's going OK. I'm terribly bored, Dad. In this apartment all by myself."

"Anthony stops by, doesn't he?"

"On most nights. But he joined that frat, so they tend to take up a lot of his time." Clara closed her eyes, thinking about the week he'd decided to pledge. She had been worried, afraid he would be forced to do something he didn't want to do. Anthony hadn't seemed fazed. He had smiled and talked about how much fun it was going to be, telling her that he was going to meet a lot of connected people. To him, the frat was a networking goldmine. All Clara saw was a lot of parties and things that could go wrong. Anthony had brushed aside her concerns, assuring her that being in the frat wouldn't change anything. From what Clara could tell, informal rush—in which the pledging was more toned down and, well, informal than it was in the spring—seemed to be a quiet affair. Given that Anthony had some prior college experience, he had been able to go through the informal rush season and had been accepted, which meant he wouldn't have to worry about rush in the spring. Still, it worried Clara more than she wanted to admit.

"A frat will be good for him. He'll be able to make connections." Her dad sounded just like Anthony. Clara rolled her eyes.

"I guess. Anyway, I had a question." A piece of her long brown hair had managed to find its way into her mouth, where she chewed on it.

"Well, spit it out. What can I do for you?"

Clara spat the hair out of her mouth and grinned. Her dad could be very direct when he thought she wanted something. "I want to intern, you know, until spring semester. And I was thinking the local precinct would be a great place to do it. Except they haven't taken on any interns in a while. I was kind of hoping that you would be able to make a phone call for me? Get my foot in the door."

The sigh on the other end of the line let her know she had him on the hook. "And what mystery are you trying to solve this time?"

"Mystery? What are you talking about?" She tried to sound as innocent as possible but she knew her dad could hear right through that.

"Clara, I offered you the chance to intern with my precinct how many times? And you always turned me down. Something must've caught your attention over there for you to decide you want to do this."

Clara bit her lip. She decided that being honest would most likely get her what she wanted. "An intern was murdered a couple years ago. A young girl, college student, lots of promise. I was thinking if I worked as an intern, I could figure out what happened to her. If I'm just an intern, people are more likely to let things slip around me, since most interns wouldn't know what they were talking about."

"Well, I'll see what I can do. I'll give the captain over there a call and ask if he'd be willing to consider you."

Clara grinned. "She, Dad. Their captain is a she."

"Got it. I'll make the call and let you know. Stay out of trouble. Love you."

"Love you too." She hung up and looked at the laptop again. Now all she could do was wait. She glanced over at the clock. It was 7 p.m. Anthony wouldn't be making an appearance tonight, it seemed. He spent more and more time at the frat, doing whatever it was they did over there, and less time with her. Clara wanted to be happy for him, but she was also jealous and sad. She went to bed, deciding that staying awake and feeling sorry for herself wouldn't accomplish anything. Clara hoped that tomorrow would be a better day.

2.

PARTY INVITE

She was an intern at the local precinct and they found her dead in the evidence locker. There was a blind spot in the security system and the killer used that to take her out. They haven't been able to solve it and I just thought I could do some poking around since I don't really have anything else to do right now." Clara took another bite of spaghetti and watched Anthony's face. He had shown up at 5, sodas in hand. Clara hadn't expected him, so she'd thrown together a quick spaghetti meal.

He nodded and took a swig of his soda. He seemed distracted, looking around at everything except her. She set down her fork and folded her arms. "What is it?"

He finally looked at her, surprise lighting up his hazel eyes. "What do you mean?"

"You've been distracted since you got here. What's up?"

He set down the soda and reached across the small table to take her hands in his. "The frat is having a party this weekend and I'd like you to come as my date. It'll be fun."

"On a Wednesday night?"

"They throw parties all nights of the week."

"Do I have to dress up?" He shook his head. "Do anything weird?" Another head shake. "OK, fine, I'll be your date. What time should I get there?"

He squeezed her hands, beaming. "The party starts at 9, so any time around then would be perfect. You're going to love it. The guys are great."

Clara smiled back, though her face felt stretched. She doubted she would 'love it' as he said, but she would give it a chance for him.

Anthony picked up his fork and shoveled in another bite. Clara watched him swallow. Clearly, he was glad she had said yes. It had seemed to relax his whole body. The tension had left his broad shoulders and the wrinkles in his high forehead had smoothed out. His taut, square jaw had loosened and a smile came more easily to his lips. She hadn't realized how nervous he'd been about asking her to go to this party.

He leaned back and rested his hands on his stomach. "So, you want to intern at the police station?"

Her mouth fell open. "You were listening?"

"Just because I had other things on my mind didn't mean I wasn't paying attention to what you were saying. I know you're bored out of your mind. I know that not being able to get into college until the spring semester is driving you crazy. And you're good at solving mysteries. Maybe this one will keep you busy for a while. And who knows? Maybe you'll figure it out and give that girl's family some closure." He took her hand again and rubbed his thumb over the top of hers. "I know I've been busy and haven't been around as much as I was before. I'm sorry for that, but this frat can open doors for me that I never thought possible. Some of these kids have really high-powered dads. An internship will keep you from being lonely." His forehead crinkled a bit. "What did you say her name was?"

"Kelly Jo. Why?"

He scratched his chin. "I think there's a shrine or something for her at the diner."

Clara's eyes lit up. "I did read that she worked there." She batted her eyelashes at him. "Mind asking around for more information about her?"

He sighed. "Anything you want. Getting this internship may even help you in the career you want to pursue."

"If my dad can get it for me." She sighed. "I hate relying on him for this kind of stuff but it's only to get my foot in the door. Everything I do from there on out will be by my own merit, not because Daddy got it for me."

Anthony nodded. "I know that. They'll figure it out pretty quickly too." He looked over at the small loveseat in front of her 32-inch TV. "How about we cuddle on the couch and you tell me more about it?"

She giggled, then jumped up to put the dishes in the sink before joining him on the loveseat, her body fitting perfectly against his.

3.

THE PARTY TO END ALL PARTIES

Clara stood in front of the full-length mirror next to her single bed, twisting and turning in all directions. If she could turn her head in a complete 360 to see the back of her outfit, she would have. "I hate parties." She groaned, knowing it was a lie. She loved parties, all the lights and decorations and music and dancing. What she hated were parties where the only person she knew would be her boyfriend and where a bunch of frat guys would be looking at her like a piece of meat all night. At least in her boot-cut jeans and dark green tube top, she wouldn't feel so exposed. After pulling on strappy sandals, she walked to the front door just as she heard a knock on it. Clara looked over at her clock, grinning. At least he was on time.

She opened the door and smiled up at him. Tonight, he had slicked back his dark hair and was wearing a beige button-up shirt, open at the collar, with dark jeans to match. "You look stunning, as usual." He leaned in for a kiss, his cologne wrapping around her as he got closer.

"And you smell amazing. Where did you get that?"

He pulled back, his eyebrows raised. "One of the guys handed out bottles last week after some event. Definitely more expensive than I would ever buy, but it was free, so." He shrugged, trying to hide how uncomfortable taking something for free made him feel.

She inhaled deeply, closing her eyes. "Smells like fresh-cut grass and the beach. Not a bad combo." She stood on tippy-toe, kissing his cheek. "Ready?"

He nodded and held out his arm for her to take. She laughed as she slipped her arm through his, then walked down the stairs with him. Anthony looked over at her elevator, which sported an "Out of Order" sign.

"Broken again?"

She shrugged. "Stairs are a good form of exercise."

Anthony just shook his head, trying to suppress the sigh that wanted to come bubbling out.

On the street, she looked for his car but didn't see it. "Are we walking there?"

Anthony held up a key fob and hit one of the buttons. Not five feet away, a brand-new, red Camaro beeped. She turned to him, her mouth falling open. He pulled open the passenger-side door and held it for her. "Ma'am?"

Clara climbed in, her mouth still hanging open. The white and red interior looked pristine, with not a speck of dirt in sight. A new-leather smell filled her nostrils until she couldn't smell anything else. She sat back, the leather conforming

17

to her body. As Anthony started the car, she turned to him. "How?"

He shrugged. "It belongs to one of the guys. He let me borrow it to come pick you up. They're always doing stuff like that, letting me borrow things. It's pretty cool." Clara could hear the gratitude in his voice and it grated on her ears. Anthony didn't need these things to be the person he was. He could be great without them. But instead of saying that, instead of starting a fight, she leaned back and let him drive. Why spoil the fun now?

When they pulled up to the house, Clara leaned against the window and looked out. The house looked older than she had anticipated, a bright blue paint job not hiding the wear. A wraparound porch and a bay window were in the front. The lawn and garden looked well cared for, although Clara doubted the boys did that themselves. They probably paid someone else to maintain it.

Anthony came around to her side and opened the door for her. "Ma'am?"

She took his hand and stepped out, looking at the flashing lights coming from inside the house. Music throbbed, causing her heartbeat to sync with it.

"We won't get in trouble, will we?"

He grinned. "Isn't that half the fun?"

She pulled her hand out of his and looked into his eyes. "Not really. Especially if I want to be an intern for the police."

He wrapped an arm around her waist and pulled her toward the house. "Nothing is going to happen. The neighbors are actually pretty cool." She looked over at the house next door, which was much newer than the frat house, white with blue trim. An upstairs curtain fluttered, but Clara couldn't make out who was behind it. Anthony turned her back to the house. "Come meet the guys."

Clara clenched her teeth, determined to get this over with as quickly as possible. Meeting the guys was definitely not something she had been looking forward to doing. In fact, it was exactly what she had been avoiding.

Anthony pulled her up the front steps, which creaked as she stepped on them. They walked through the open front door and into an entrance hall covered with confetti and banners, then through a hallway that led to a large living room with a fireplace against the far wall. Across from the fireplace was a bay window, where people stood next to each other, barely leaving any room to get by. Near the fireplace stood four boys, all about the same height and build, holding red Solo cups and talking. All four wore polo shirts in varying colors with jeans and sneakers. Clara decided that she would just assign them a shirt color to remember who they were. Anthony pulled her up to them, smiling as widely as he could. "Hey, guys. This is Clara, my girlfriend."

All four turned to her, their eyebrows shooting up.

"So, she does exist." The guy in the red shirt smiled down at her, his sandy blonde hair swept away from his forehead and his green eyes scrunched in the corner with his smile. He even had dimples in both cheeks.

"That's rude, Darren." The guy in the yellow shirt made to hit Red Shirt and Clara smiled. Yellow Shirt had black hair, with dark eyes to match. In the right light, they looked black, too. With his straight nose and square chin, he looked very much like a fairytale prince.

"He's just making an observation, Charlie."

Yellow Shirt shook his head.

Green Shirt, who had responded, stuck out his hand to shake hers. "Name's Warren. So stuffy, I know. Most people just call me Jay." Clara shook his hand, surprised to find it warm and his handshake firm. His blonde hair had been cut close to his head, so no fancy styles for him. He gave her a lopsided grin, revealing only one dimple in his cheek, a pointed chin, and high cheekbones. Clara couldn't decide whether his eyes were blue or green, as they kept changing.

"Don't hog her, Jay." The fourth boy, in a black shirt, took her hand from Green Shirt and brought it to his lips, kissing the back. The other three boys whistled. Anthony shifted uncomfortably next to Clara, and Clara pulled her hand back to her chest as quickly as possible, her ears burning. Black Shirt bowed slightly, his shoulder-length brown hair falling into his hazel eyes. His beaming smile was so disarming, Clara had to remind herself that she didn't like these guys.

Sticking her hands behind her back, Clara turned to Green Shirt. "So, why Jay? Warren and Jay are so different."

He scratched the back of his neck, laughing. "Well, my middle name is James, but we already had two of those when I joined the frat and I didn't want to be 'James the Third' or some nonsense, so I decided to go by Jay. Been that way ever since. Drives the folks nuts." He winked at her, bringing back the burning ears again.

She tilted her head, smiling. "So, did you all meet here, in the frat?"

Red Shirt and Yellow Shirt exchanged glances. "No. Charlie and I grew up together. We pledged together and both got in." Red Shirt clapped Yellow on the back, making his drink tip and dribble a little over the edge of his cup. Noticing her look at the drink, Yellow Shirt smiled.

"Beer?"

Clara wrinkled her nose and shook her head. "No thanks. I'm not old enough."

The four exchanged glances, then looked at Anthony.

"Her dad's a cop, guys." All four cups ended up closer to their bodies. If they could have, they probably would've absorbed them into their chests.

Clara smiled. "Don't worry, I'm not a tattletale. I just don't like the stuff to begin with, so sneaking some has never been of interest to me."

Black Shirt quirked an eyebrow. "If you don't drink it, how do you know you don't like the taste?" He nudged Green Shirt with his elbow, proud of his observation.

"Oh, I never said I've never had any. I did, once. It had to be the grossest thing I've ever tasted. So now I don't even bother."

Anthony placed his hand on her back and turned her away. "We have more to drink than just beer. Let's grab some punch." He waved at the guys as he steered her toward the kitchen.

The kitchen ended up having two fridges, a stove, and a dishwasher, all in stainless steel. The counters were dark granite and the cupboards were made of dark wood. A huge punch bowl sat on the island. Anthony grabbed a cup and filled it to the brim with bright red punch. He took a long swallow, closing his eyes. He turned to Clara, offering her the cup. She took it, taking only a small sip. While she believed Anthony would never give her alcohol on purpose, that didn't mean someone else hadn't spiked the punch. She decided to switch it out for water the first chance she got.

He leaned his hip against the counter and smiled at her. "So, what did you think?"

"They're interesting. The one with the short hair, in the green shirt? Is he military?"

"He plans to be. Wants to finish college and join the Marines, if you can believe that." Anthony smiled and reached over to touch her hair. "You look so pretty tonight."

She took his hand in hers and pressed it to her cheek. "Thanks. And, yes, I believe it. He has that kind of bearing."

Anthony leaned forward, arching his eyebrows. "And what do you know of military bearing, young lady?" The laugh in his voice was infectious.

Clara giggled. "Dad was military, remember? Before he became a cop."

Anthony clapped a hand on his forehead in the most dramatic pose he could muster. "Oh, that's right. I completely forgot." He dragged out the last syllable, opening one eye to look at her. Clara bent over in a fit of giggles, unable to contain herself.

"You're a goof."

He straightened up and placed both hands on the counter. "I just love to see you smile." He looked past her, at something behind her. "They're good guys. Maybe a little spoiled, and they like to joke, but good guys." Clara could hear the persistence in his voice, his almost pleading with her to believe him. After having met them, she couldn't deny that they had been very nice to her, even joking around to ease her discomfort. Maybe they weren't as bad as she had believed them to be.

Clara wrapped an arm around Anthony's waist and looked up at him. "So, now what do we do?"

He gestured toward the back door. "There is a world of fun out there, milady. What would you like to do? We have games, music, anything."

She scratched her chin, pretending to think. "Let's play games! That sounds fun."

Anthony grabbed her hand and pulled her back into the living room. A game of charades was just starting, so they joined in. Only after the fact did Clara realize that the four boys had joined them. They split into teams of two, with Anthony claiming Clara before anyone else could. Green Shirt and Yellow Shirt teamed up together, leaving Red and Black to team up together. Clara watched as they tore up small pieces of paper with words written on them, then tossed them into a baseball cap and mixed them up.

Black Shirt held the hat out to Clara. "Ladies first."

She looked at the two other girls who were playing, on the same team together, although Clara suspected that if one of the boys had asked, the girls would've split immediately. She shrugged and took a slip of paper off the top.

Dog had been hastily scribbled on the paper. Clara stood by the fireplace and turned to Anthony. Knowing she couldn't make any noise, she got down on all fours and lolled her tongue. Anthony, sitting on the couch across from her, leaned forward with his elbows on his knees, watching her. She took four steps, lapped her tongue out again, and looked at him. He grinned. "Dog!"

Clara nodded, getting to her feet. She looked at the boys, who were all staring at her with slightly surprised looks on their faces.

"Um, why didn't you guys guess?"

Green Shirt responded first, blinking several times. "We play it a little differently here. Since we usually play during a party, we give the team time to guess the answer first. Then, if they can't get what their partner is doing, the rest can jump in." To Clara's ears, it sounded like a total lie. Even the look Anthony gave him seemed full of confusion.

Clara sat down next to Anthony and looked at the boys. "Well, who's next?"

Black Shirt reached into the hat and pulled out a slip of paper. He went up to the fireplace, bouncing back and forth like a bunny. Red Shirt kept throwing out the most random words he could think of, while Anthony sat next to her, tapping her knee with his fingers. He knew the answer and not being able to shout it out was killing him. Red Shirt finally gave up and Anthony cried out, "Bunny!" Black Shirt nodded and sat back down.

By the time Clara looked at her watch, Anthony had gotten them a solid lead. They would have to lose the next four rounds for anyone else to even come close to catching them. Clara yawned, realizing that it was close to midnight. She was exhausted, her whole body deflating. Anthony noticed the yawn and looked at his watch, too. "I better get you home." He stood and pulled her to her feet. "I just gotta drive Clara home, guys, then I'll be back." The four boys nodded, each standing up to shake her hand, which Clara, in her exhaustion, found kind of funny. Then Anthony led her out the door and to the borrowed car. As he helped her inside, he asked, "Did you have fun?"

She smiled up at him. "I did. They really do seem nice, just like you said."

His grin quickened her heartbeat. He looked so happy, his whole face lighting up at her answer. "I'm glad."

The drive back to the apartment was quiet, as Clara was barely able to keep her eyes open. At one point, she heard a snore, which jolted her out of her sleep. Anthony looked over at her, one eyebrow raised.

"I'm snoring, aren't I?"

"Like a lumberjack." His grin grew even wider.

"Don't laugh. I'm just really tired. I swear I don't snore all the time."

He shrugged. "Doesn't bother me. I know I snore."

At her apartment, he walked her up to her door. "Thank you for a lovely night." She leaned in for a kiss only to find that he was doing so as well. Anthony pressed her against her door, his fingers running through her hair, sending shivers down her spine.

"I'm so glad you came. And that you had fun." A second kiss sent another jolt down her spine. She pushed him back, her lips tingling.

"I did. But I'm really tired. Call you tomorrow?"

He nodded and then kissed the top of her head before walking back to the car.

Clara entered her apartment and pulled the door closed behind her, leaning against it. Blowing out her breath, she tried to slow her racing heart. He could definitely kiss. She grinned and took those kisses to bed with her, falling asleep to the feel of his lips on hers.

4.

THE INTERNSHIP

The next morning, a pealing sound woke Clara from a deep sleep. She knew she had been dreaming because when the pealing had first started, she had assumed it was part of the dream, even though as soon as her eyes popped open, the only thing she could remember was the dead intern's face imprinted on her mind. Another peal sounded, making her realize that the sound was coming from her bedside table, where her phone lay on top of a Bluetooth charger. Groaning, she pulled it to her face and hit the answer button. "Yes?"

"Is that any way to greet your father?" Her dad's voice on the other end was full of sunshine and rainbows. Clara looked at her clock, which read 7 a.m.

"Dad, it's only 6 a.m. over there. How are you so chipper this early in the morning?"

"Coffee, sweetie, lots of good coffee."

She groaned again, then rolled out of bed and headed for the kitchen. "Guess I'll get some myself. So, what's up?"

"You got the internship."

Clara almost dropped the phone in the sink. She pulled it tighter to her face. "I did?"

He chuckled, the phone shaking with the vibration of it. "Of course you did. I explained to the captain that you had taken an interest in the previous intern's death and informed her that you wanted to intern yourself and learn the ropes, while also seeing if you could learn anything else, maybe hear things that they missed."

"And she was OK with that?" Clara held her breath, waiting for the conditions she was sure would come with the opportunity.

"More than OK. This is a big black mark on her precinct. A murder happens in their house and they can't solve it? That looks bad. It's been two years since that poor girl died and the captain is determined to figure out who did it. She agreed with your theory that people tend to ignore interns and thought it would be good to have an extra set of ears around. Her only thing is, you have to report directly to her and if you notice anything suspicious, you are not to pursue it alone."

Clara smiled. "That sounds like my father talking more than the police captain."

He chuckled again. "I may have told her those were my rules for you being allowed to work with them. She agreed."

"Dad, this is amazing! When do I start?"

"In an hour. So, you better get moving."

Clara squealed and thanked him, then rushed into the bathroom to get ready. She pulled her dark brown hair into a bun at the nape of her neck, grabbed black slacks and a dark blue button-up top, and tossed on a pair of black flats. She considered her black boots, but decided against them, at least for her first day. She quickly applied eyeliner and mascara, not bothering with anything else. A quick brush of her teeth, then she grabbed a travel mug and filled it with coffee, adding some honey and stirring as she headed to the door. She grabbed her purse, slung it over her shoulder, and hurried out to her car.

Behind the wheel, she shot Anthony a quick text, telling him that she had again enjoyed the previous night and that she had gotten the internship. She told him that it started today and because she knew he had the night off, she suggested they grab dinner out to celebrate. Then, she put her phone in her purse and headed to the precinct, excited to start her first day there. Finally, she would be doing something useful.

Clara took a deep breath as she pulled into the precinct parking lot. Not exactly sure where to park her poor little car, she finally settled on a spot near the back. For two summers before her senior year, she had saved up to buy the vehicle, then had ended up having to drive it north when they moved. While it ran pretty well, it wasn't exactly the most beautiful car to behold. Tan leather interior, silver plastic trim, the radio didn't even make phone calls like newer cars. But her little red Mazda ran as well as could be expected. Clara headed to the front of the precinct, not sure where she was supposed to go. She kicked herself for not asking her dad that.

The front of the building had seen better days. The entrance had an arch that at one time may have been pretty and regal-looking but that now had peeling paint and chunks missing from it. Up close, Clara could see that someone had attempted to paint it, going from its original tan to a dark brown, but the tan had started to show through in spots. Concrete steps led up to the front door, where a ramp ascended from the side to enable handicap access. The doors were all glass. Through them, Clara could see metal detectors. Clara stepped inside, didn't set anything off, and then walked up to the front desk. The lobby was sparse, with no potted plants or anything to brighten it up. Just a row of benches to one side, an elevator to the left, a sign pointing to restrooms around the corner, and a lone reception desk. Everything was decorated in browns and greens, and brown tile covered the floor.

As Clara walked in, the officer at the desk looked up and eyed her. The woman couldn't have been much older than Clara. Her blonde hair was pulled back in a severe bun and glasses covered her dark brown eyes. She pushed them up her thin nose and looked into Clara's eyes. "Can I help you?"

Clara placed both hands on the desk, smiling her biggest smile. The officer didn't respond. "Um, yes. I'm here to see the captain. I'm the new intern."

The officer scoffed. "We don't have interns at this precinct."

"You haven't had interns for two years, I know. But that's changing. I'm here to help."

The officer crossed her arms over her uniform and leaned back in the chair. "We've been just fine for the last two years without one. Why would we need one now?"

Clara spread her fingers and chewed on her bottom lip. "Can I please see the captain?"

The officer looked at the clock on the wall behind her. "Captain's busy. Sorry."

Clara dug her fingers into the top of the desk. This wasn't going how she had expected at all. Steeling herself for a fight, she opened her mouth only to hear from behind, "Officer Livingston, I'll take Ms. Young. Thank you."

The officer frowned and turned away from Clara.

Clara turned around and came face to face with one of the most beautiful women she had ever met. The woman was tall and had ebony skin. Her hair was shaved close to her head and her hazel eyes seemed more yellow than brown. Wearing a brown pantsuit, the captain of this precinct cut a nice figure. She held out her hand, which Clara shook with enthusiasm. "Very nice to meet you, ma'am. I'm Clara."

The captain smiled. "Captain Bailey. Your dad spoke pretty highly of you." Captain Bailey led Clara to the elevators and pressed the up button.

"That's his job, to brag about his kids." Clara grinned, feeling her smile stretch her face. "I have a semester off and was hoping to help out around the precinct, do anything your officers haven't had time to do. I'm pretty good at paperwork."

Captain Bailey led Clara past a room full of cubicles, each desk adorned with a phone, a computer, and two chairs, as though the partners all shared the desks. Here, the brown and green concept had infected the carpet as well as the walls. Fans overhead whooshed in a steady beat. Captain Bailey opened the door to her office, one of three against the far wall. When Clara stepped in, she smiled. The brown and green were completely gone, as the office had been decorated in gentle colors. The walls were white, with blue trim around the big window. In the middle of the room sat a desk with bookshelves flanking it. A chair had been positioned against the wall, while two chairs sat in front of the desk. Clara took one of the chairs, smiling at the captain again. "And learning information?" the captain asked.

Clara nodded. "Interns don't get noticed. People may say things around me that they won't say around you. I may be able to learn more about what happened to Kelly Jo."

"What do you know about her?"

Clara shrugged. "Just what I read online. But no one deserves to have their murder unsolved. Her killer needs to be found."

The captain leaned back in her chair, her fingers touching under her chin. "She worked in Evidence, helping catalog everything. We've been switching from handwritten to digital for a while, and she was inputting everything into the computer. Since her death, we really haven't gotten back around to finishing that project, so I'm going to leave that to you. You won't be getting coffee or running errands for the officers. You're here to work in Evidence. Got it?"

Her words came out very forceful, causing Clara to take notice. "Is that what happened to Kelly Jo?"

The captain sighed. "When she first started, they gave her a hard time. Nothing serious, but the first week they had her running around like a chicken with her head cut off, getting them coffee, taking notes from one end of the precinct to the other. Nothing dangerous or demeaning but she was exhausted by the end of the week and I didn't think she would stick around. To keep her here, I moved her to Evidence and set her up cataloging everything. I don't want them to take advantage of you, so we aren't even going to give them that chance."

Clara nodded. "I get it. But I'm not her. I've grown up around police my entire life. I wouldn't let them take advantage of me."

Captain Bailey nodded and stood. "Good. Let me take you to Evidence. You have a lot of work ahead of you. Kelly Jo had only just started when she died."

The captain led Clara out of the office and back to the elevators. As Clara stepped inside, she glanced back at the room of cubicles. Several cops were looking around the cubicle walls at her, sizing her up. Lifting her chin, she winked at them, knowing it would do the most to unnerve them. Plus, it showed confidence.

As the doors slid closed, one cop winked back, catching Clara's eye. Before the doors had completely shut, she saw a shock of red hair against pale skin, freckles, and a toothy grin. Clara blinked and turned to Captain Bailey, trying to figure out how to ask who that cop was.

Before she got the chance, the doors were open again and they were walking down a dark corridor, past several closed doors. "Interrogation. Nothing fancy. Each room mirrors another with the two-way viewing so we can watch the suspects." The captain stopped in front of the last door at the end of the hall. It looked like all the others—dark wood with a window, blinds pulled closed. However, instead of numbers on the glass, the word "Evidence" had been stamped. Captain Bailey pushed open the door and gestured for Clara to head inside.

Sitting at the desk outside the caged evidence locker was an older black man with eyes of steel. They locked onto Clara as soon as she stepped into the room, freezing her in place. He seemed to be assessing her before making a decision. Then he nodded up at the captain. The man stood and held out a hand. "Ma'am, good morning. How can I help you?" His voice came out gruff and clipped.

Captain Bailey shook his hand with both of hers, his engulfing her own. "Morgan, this is Clara Young. She's going to be interning here with us and helping you catalog all this evidence." She looked over at the computer on the second desk. It wasn't even turned on.

Morgan ran a hand over the back of his neck, his shoulders slumping just a little. "I'm sorry I haven't gotten further. Computers and I just don't get along." At his full height, he towered over both women, although Clara didn't get the sense that he was looking down on them the way she did with some people. The steel in his eyes softened just a bit when he caught her looking at him. He ran one large hand over his bald head and gave her a tight smile.

"I'm pretty handy with computers. I can usually make them do what I need them to do," Clara said. "Where do you want me to start?"

He took a key from the belt around his waist and walked to the cage, limping on his left leg. Clara looked to Captain Bailey, but she shook her head, leaving no room for questions. Morgan came back with two boxes, which he set down on the second desk. "This should be a good place to start. Like I said, I haven't gotten very far." He sat back down at the other desk, the chair creaking under his weight.

Captain Bailey nodded to them both, then left without another word. Clara opened the first box, which was coated with dust. Inside, she found stacks of files, the paper yellowed with age. "Some of those records go back 50 years, so be careful." With a swig of his coffee, Morgan turned back to the newspaper in front of him, leaving her to herself.

Clara booted up the computer and found the spreadsheet that Kelly Jo had started two years ago. She had been very thorough, separating the crimes into categories. Each category had a sheet for each individual crime. Clara spent the better part of the morning working her way through half the box, dividing the files into the smaller crimes like petty theft and the bigger crimes like murder. Because the contents of this box were older, there wasn't much to file besides the officers' notes.

By lunchtime, Clara had filled four spreadsheets with information from the files. She leaned back in the chair and stretched her arms over her head. Morgan had gone from the newspaper to a crossword puzzle book, in which he was writing his answers in pencil. Clara stood and walked across the room to stretch her legs. She looked over Morgan's shoulder and realized that it was a cop crossword puzzle book, with every clue relating to police officers. "That's a cool book. Where did you get it?"

He glanced up at her, his forehead wrinkled. His nose flared and she backed up a step, holding up both hands.

"I'm sorry, I didn't mean to intrude. It's just that my dad loves stuff like that, so I thought I could get him one."

He set the book down and turned his full attention to her. "And what would your dad know about doing cop crossword puzzles?"

Clara shrugged, grinning. "Just that he's a cop and he likes crosswords."

Morgan's eyes hardened as he stared at her, but Clara wouldn't let him intimidate her. She raised her chin and met his gaze with one of her own. "Where does your dad work?"

The question caught her off-guard, making her stutter. "Uh, in, uh, Pennsylvania." She swallowed. "He used to work in Florida, but he moved us out to Pennsylvania when a better opportunity presented itself." She leaned against the desk and crossed her arms. "What about you? Where did you start off?"

"Here in this very precinct. Been here my whole career."

Clara nodded, straightening up.

"Love this precinct. They're my family, even if they do forget I'm here sometimes."

Before Clara could respond, the door flew open and two cops walked in, laughing. "Morgan, are you hungry?" The older of the two talked with a bellow, like every word had to be shouted. With a thinning hairline and a protruding belly, he looked like a stereotypical cop. The buttons on his uniform top seemed to be stretched a little tight. He clapped his partner on the back, almost sending the kid sprawling. Unlike the older cop, the kid couldn't have weighed more than Clara, as tall and thin as he was. His hair had been cut so close to his head, he looked almost bald. "Harry's buying today. He lost a bet."

Morgan stood and walked around the desk to meet them. "A bet? Harry, what did you let him talk you into?"

The younger man, Harry, shrugged. "I swear I didn't mean to. He just bet that he could guess how fast the cars were going. I didn't believe him. He was right, every time."

The older cop pulled up his pants by the belt and smiled. "When you do this long enough, you just know. Right, Morgan?"

Morgan shook his head. "Harry, no more betting Ralph. He wins every time." Morgan looked at Clara over his shoulder. "Going to grab lunch. You coming?"

Clara grabbed her purse from the drawer in the desk and followed them out, watching as Morgan locked the door behind him. "How many people have keys to the evidence room?"

Morgan looked at her, his hand halfway back to his pocket. "Just me and the captain. For security purposes." He looked to where the guys were waiting for them by the elevator. "There's a food truck downstairs. Comes every day. That's usually where we eat." He headed to the elevators without waiting for Clara to reply. She scrambled after him, not wanting to be left alone in the corridor.

Down at the food truck, which had parked in the far right corner of the precinct's parking lot, Clara ordered two tacos and a soda. She watched as other cops came and went, taking their food back inside with them. Morgan and his buddies stayed outside, sitting on the benches at the front of the precinct and enjoying the warm afternoon sun. Clara considered joining them but decided against it. Instead, she sat on a patch of grass under a tree to the right of the precinct entrance. Leaning against the tree, she closed her eyes for a moment, letting her senses take over. The smell of tacos and car fumes permeated the air but under that she could smell soil and flowers from the bushes nearby.

She opened her eyes to find a red-haired officer standing in front of her, taco and drink in hand. "Did I wake you? I can leave."

Clara shook her head. "No, I'm awake. Just enjoying a moment of peace. Of course you can join me."

He sat next to her and crossed his long legs. His red hair had been combed to the side and was plastered to his head with spray and gel. Freckles dotted his long nose and high cheeks, giving his face a youthful look—an effect that became even more pronounced when he smiled and a dimple appeared in his right cheek. If Clara had to guess, she'd peg him at under 30 years old. He took a bite of taco, watching her watch him. After a big swallow, he asked, "Are you going to eat at all or just watch me?"

Her eyes widened and her cheeks reddened. "Sorry." She took a bite. The taco was cool and crisp, but spicy at the same time. "Wow, these are pretty good."

He nodded. "Yeah, we wouldn't keep asking them to come back if they weren't." The cop turned to her again, smiling. "How do you like working with Morgan?"

Clara looked over at Morgan, who was leaning against the wall behind the bench, his eyes closed against the midday sun. "He's quiet. Keeps to himself, mostly. Really hasn't talked to me all morning."

"Don't take it personally. That's Morgan. He's sizing you up, deciding whether he likes you or not. He invited you down here, which means he doesn't outright dislike you."

Clara turned her attention back to the cop at her side. "What do you mean?"

He grinned, revealing a piece of lettuce stuck in his perfect white teeth. "The last person they assigned to help him? A rookie? Morgan let him eat his packed lunch for three days before telling him about the food truck. And since the poor kid didn't talk to anyone else for those three days, he didn't know he was missing out."

"How did he find out?"

"Followed Morgan out here one afternoon after realizing that he had to be getting food from somewhere."

Clara took another bite and thought about her next question. "How did Morgan react?"

"He laughed, congratulated the kid on being a decent cop, and bought him lunch." The cop pointed to the skinny kid, Harry. "It was Carver." At Clara's confused look, the cop pointed at the younger cop sitting next to Morgan. "Harry."

Clara's eyebrows shot up. "So, he used to work in Evidence with Morgan?"

"Not for very long. Only long enough for Morgan to decide he'd be better off out on the streets and to convince the captain to move him."

Clara leaned back against the tree and crumpled up her empty taco wrapper. "Wow. He did all that for Harry?"

"Of course he did. That's the kind of guy Morgan is. He's tough, but once you gain his trust, he'll bend over backward for you." The cop wiped his hand on a napkin, then extended the hand out to Clara. "I'm Will, by the way."

Clara shook his hand, surprised to find his fingers so cold. "Clara. I'm the new intern."

"Ah, so you're the girl. You have a lot of work ahead of you."

"Is it that bad?" Clara opened her second taco and took a large bite.

He scratched his chin. "Well, maybe not horrible, but you're going to be busy for a very long time. I'll be surprised if you even get halfway through those files before your internship is up."

After finishing the second taco, Clara looked back toward the precinct. "I'm going to get them all done. Otherwise, what's the point of my being here?"

"To get experience? Have something to do? Receive college credit?" He said these lightly, but Clara could hear the question in his voice. He wanted to know why she was at the precinct.

"All of the above." While the captain knew that Clara was looking for clues to Kelly Jo's death, that didn't mean the other cops had to know. The less attention they paid to her, the better.

Will nodded, seeming to accept her answer without question. He stood and brushed off his pants. "Time to get back to work. Nice chatting with you." He walked back toward the precinct, whistling a tune to himself. Clara watched him go, curious to know why he had sat next to her in the first place.

5.

DINNER CELEBRATION

Clara rushed into the restaurant, feeling like a fool. She was the one who had suggested they go out to dinner to celebrate her internship, and now she was the one who was late. She had gotten so caught up in cataloging that she had forgotten to keep an eye on the time. She had left only because Morgan had asked her how long she planned to stay, causing her to realize how late it had gotten. Clara had thanked him as she rushed out of the room, her purse slung over one shoulder.

Anthony sat at a table near the back, his starched white shirt looking like a beacon in the dark. With his dark hair styled, he looked like a modern-day Romeo. Clara slipped into the seat across from him, apologies flying from her lips. "I'm so sorry, Anthony. I lost track of time. There's so much evidence to catalog. Kelly Jo didn't even make a dent. She barely got the spreadsheets set up."

He smiled, but the expression didn't reach his eyes. He tapped his fingers on the table, almost in time with her pounding heart. "So, you really want to go through with this?"

"With what? The internship? Isn't that what we're celebrating tonight? That I got it?"

"That's what you're celebrating. I'm here to support you." He took a sip of water and looked away.

"Anthony, what's wrong? Why are you upset?"

He sighed. "I'm not upset. I'm just stressed and when I got your message, it stressed me out even more. You're investigating another murderer." He held up his hand before she could protest. "It occurred to me after I got your message that this was for real going to happen. When you were talking about it last night, it was just talk. Now that you have the internship, I'm worried."

Clara bit her lip and tried to see his point of view. Granted, it was dangerous, but being a cop was dangerous. "Anthony, what do you think I want to do with my life?"

He waved a hand in the air. "Go to college, graduate, get a corporate job, get married, have kids, grow old with me." He gave her his most charming smile—the smile that had won her over in the first place.

"While those are good things, the corporate thing really isn't what I want to do. I want to be a cop like my dad. Like my brother." Clara fidgeted with the white tablecloth, pulling a loose string on the trim. "I've always wanted to be a cop. I thought you knew that. I'm going to study criminal justice in the spring."

"You really are serious about that?" As he said this, a waiter appeared at his elbow, asking if they knew what they wanted. The waiter wore black slacks and a white top. Clara realized that

Anthony was dressed almost identically. It seemed odd, but she brushed it off. It was just a coincidence.

Anthony looked down at the menu in front of him. "I'll have the fish tacos. Clara?"

Clara sighed. "Can I get the guacamole burger, please? With fries?" The waiter nodded, took the menus, and went to put in their orders. Clara took a sip of water to distract herself.

Anthony leaned forward and reached for her free hand. "Look, I just want you to realize that the path you're choosing is really dangerous. And that I worry about you."

"Anthony, you have to realize, I'm really good at this. I've been listening to my dad do it my whole life. It's second nature for me." She took his hand and squeezed it. "What I did back home, that wasn't just a fluke. I've done it before."

"You've solved other murders?" The question came out with more consternation then he had intended and his face immediately reflected it. Clara nodded.

"Yes. First time was when I was twelve. I notice things other people don't. I always have."

They sat in silence as the waiter brought their food and let them know the plates were hot. Clara thanked him, smiling up into his tired face. He couldn't have been much older than Anthony, but he looked exhausted, with heavy bags under his blue eyes.

Anthony dug into his taco while Clara doused her fries in ketchup. "I met a couple of the officers today," she said.

He looked up, swallowing. "Oh yeah? How did that go?"

"They were nice. The one who works in Evidence isn't sure about me yet but I'm positive I can win him over. He has two friends who come get him for lunch. And another officer ate lunch with me today. Very welcoming." She took a bite of the burger, savoring the mix of creamy avocado and charcoal tang.

"Well, at least that's a plus. Maybe you'll make some work friends."

At the mention of friends, Clara's shoulders drooped. She was reminded of her friends from Pennsylvania. Tracy, Hannah, and Stacy had been the first girls to take any interest in Clara when she had enrolled in her new school during her senior year. Hannah had been a little standoffish at first, seeing as how her dad had lost the last sheriff's election to Clara's dad. However, after Clara had opened up to them about what she was finding in relation to the death of a student who had been close to Hannah, Hannah had opened up to accepting Clara. Once that happened, the four had become inseparable.

Anthony noticed the look on her face and stopped eating. He set down his taco. "I'm sorry. I didn't mean to say that you needed new friends. I just don't like seeing you so lonely."

Clara sighed. "I know. I just miss them." She finished her burger, ready to go to bed. This dinner wasn't what she'd had in mind earlier that morning, when she had thought about celebrating. "I think I'm just going to go home. It's been a long day and I'm tired." She stood up and pulled cash out of her purse.

Anthony reached out a hand to stop her. "My treat, for you. Celebrating, remember?" She nodded and turned to walk out of the restaurant. Before she had taken two steps, his arms had wrapped around her from behind. He pulled her to his chest. "I know this is hard. I know it's not what you thought it would be. But it'll get better, OK? We'll get into a routine and get things worked out."

Clara nodded, her head rubbing against his chest. She inhaled the scent of pine. She smelled something else underneath—something she recognized but couldn't place. "I really do need to go home. Thanks for dinner." She leaned back for a kiss and accepted the soft one he planted on her lips. Then she rushed out, ducking her head as she did.

Once home in her bed, Clara pulled out her journal from her

nightstand. "Got the internship, YAY! Anthony isn't as happy as I thought he'd be. He seems worried about my safety, of all things. Doesn't seem happy that I want to be a cop as a career. What did he think I was going to college for? Then he mentioned friends and I just got all sad and ruined the night. I miss the girls. I wish they were here. I'll have to call them tomorrow." Clara put the journal back in its drawer and shut off the light, hoping the next day would be better.

6.

CATCHING UP

The next morning, while brushing her teeth, Clara called Stacy. "Stace, how have you been?"

The groggy voice on the other end of the line gurgled a response.

Clara adjusted the volume on her phone and spit out the minty toothpaste. "Earth to Stacy, wake up. Don't you have a class soon?"

There was a clatter and a shout. "Oh goodness, Clara, I'm going to be late. Thank you for waking me. How did you know?"

Clara giggled. "I didn't. I just had a feeling I needed to call you."

"Well, you, sister, are a lifesaver. This professor hates it when people are late. Why didn't my alarm go off?" Clara could hear Stacy rummaging around her room, tossing books and pulling on clothes.

"Stacy, what have you been up to?"

There was a pause in the movement on the other end of the line. "Oh, nothing really. Just school mostly. Studying takes up most of my time. And Rodney." There was a pause, like Stacy was holding her breath.

"Stacy, are you getting serious with my older brother?" Clara tried to sound tough, but couldn't keep the smile from her lips. Her best friend and her brother dating had been partly her idea.

Stacy giggled. "If seeing him every weekend I go home is serious, then yes." Clara heard a door bang on the other end of the line. "Hey, girl, loved the chat but I have to run. Talk later?"

"Of course! Good luck in class." Clara hung up and headed to the kitchen to grab her purse off the counter. She slipped on her flats, then walked to the door.

Once out in her car, she dialed Tracy and put it on speakerphone. Tracy picked up on the third ring. She sounded more awake than Stacy had. As she drove to the precinct, Clara could see Tracy's bright red hair in her mind's eye. "Tracy! What are you up to this fine morning?"

"Oh, Clara, I'm just working on a project. School's just started and they're already running me ragged. This is what I get for trying to be so smart."

"Trying to be! You're smart. What are you talking about?" Clara turned a corner and the precinct came into sight.

"Yeah, well, some of these professors can really make you feel dumb. I'm trying to not get discouraged. What about you? What have you been doing? Settled into the apartment?"

"I am. It's nice and cozy. You girls should come down for a weekend."

On the other end of the line, Tracy clapped her hands. "Oh, that would be wonderful. We'll have to coordinate that for sure." Clara heard what sounded like a chip crunch in the background. "How's Anthony?"

"He's doing well. Got into that frat I told you about. Still not sure about those guys. I've met them but I don't know. Frats really aren't my thing." Clara parked the car in the same corner where she'd parked the day before. Mentally, she dubbed it "her spot."

"But frat guys are fun! And they have great parties and so many events." Tracy's voice took on a defensive edge, piquing Clara's interest.

"Tracy, are you dating a frat guy?"

Tracy snorted. "How did you even guess that?"

"By the way you started defending them. You gave yourself away! You have to tell me about him!"

Another chip crunched on the line. "He's gorgeous and funny and his smile is so dreamy. And he's smart, if you can believe that about a frat guy.

Anyway, I'll fill you in later. Right now I have to get cracking on this project."

Clara looked at her dash clock. "Yeah, I gotta get inside. I got an internship at the local precinct."

Tracy paused in mid-chip, making Clara stop moving, too. "There's more to this, isn't there? I can hear it in your voice. You found something. You'll have to tell me what it is when we talk later, OK?"

Clara laughed, the sound filling her car. "OK. I'll give you all the details later only if you promise to tell me more about your frat boy."

"Deal. Talk to you later, girlie."

Clara hung up and slipped out of her car. As she walked toward the entrance, she noticed Will heading her way.

"Good morning!" He raised a hand in greeting and Clara responded in kind. "Will, how are you?"

He fell into step beside her. "Well-rested, ready for another wonderful day."

She gave him a sideways glance. "You're mighty chipper in the morning."

He grinned. "Yeah, the guys hate it. It's wonderful." He held the door open for her as she stepped inside. Then Will glanced at the front desk. "Morning, Alice. Fine day, isn't it?"

"Couldn't be better, Will." Alice didn't even acknowledge Clara. She simply returned to the screen in front of her.

On the elevator, Clara turned to Will. "What does Alice have against me?"

He shrugged. "She feels threatened? She's not the only pretty girl around here anymore."

Clara snorted. "Pretty girl? I don't think that's it. Alice seems like the kind of girl who knows she's pretty and doesn't feel threatened by anyone."

Will shrugged. "Beats me. Alice is usually cool with everyone." He quirked an eyebrow at Clara. "Did you say anything that may have upset her?"

Clara folded her arms across her chest. "So it's my fault she doesn't like me?"

Will took a step back. "No. I'm just trying to help."

Clara shook her head. "It's OK. It really doesn't matter, anyway. Not like I'll see her very much up in Evidence." At that, the elevator chimed and the doors opened to reveal the cubicle-lined squad room. Will stepped out, smiling as he passed her.

"Lunch again today? I brought a towel we could lay on the grass."

Clara nodded. "Sounds great. See you then." The doors closed, leaving her to her own thoughts. For some reason, Alice didn't like her, but Clara couldn't figure out why.

Clara found the evidence room empty, with no sign of Morgan anywhere. Then she saw the cup of steaming coffee on his desk and figured he must've stepped out. Given the issues they'd had with security, that seemed odd. Clara slid to her desk and booted up the computer. Yesterday had been mundane work, to get a head start on the files. Today, she was going to go through the files that Kelly Jo had cataloged, to see if something inside them had gotten her killed. Maybe Kelly Jo had seen something in those files that someone didn't want anyone to know about.

Her hands itching to get started, Clara clicked open the spreadsheet, only to find it blank. All her work from the day before had been erased. She clicked through to find that anything Kelly Jo had entered had also been erased. Clara clicked through every file she could find on the computer, mumbling under her breath about technology and how useless it was. She was so lost in anger that she didn't even notice that Morgan had come back into the room until he was leaning over her shoulder, looking at the empty spreadsheet. "Lost everything, didn't you?"

Clara jumped, almost hitting the top of her head on his chin. She spun around and looked up at him, her head tilting back farther than she thought it could go. "Yes, I did. How is that even possible? I saved it repeatedly throughout the day."

"I told you, something's wrong with that computer. I've tried cataloging that particular box three times already. Every night I save it, every morning I come in to find it all deleted. Either we have a ghost who doesn't like that box or we have a mole."

Clara leaned away from him and narrowed her eyes. She felt like Morgan was testing her, but she didn't know why. "A mole? Like, someone is coming in at night and deleting the files on purpose?"

He nodded and stepped away from her, giving her some space. "I don't believe in ghosts, Ms. Young, so a mole is the only logical explanation."

"But you said yesterday that only you and Captain Bailey have the keys to get in here. So, if there is a mole, how are they getting into the room to get to the computer?"

He smirked. "The lock can be picked, you know."

She nodded, following his train of thought. "But there are cameras, especially after Kelly Jo's death. Someone would've seen whether anyone had picked the lock to get in here."

He pointed a long finger at her and smiled. "Bingo. So, how else would they get in here?"

"Duplicate key? There are already two. Who's to say they didn't take Captain Bailey's key and make a copy?" Clara decided not to suggest that someone had taken his key, as that definitely wouldn't endear her to him.

"Very perceptive. If they had a key, it would look like they belonged here. And while the captain is an outstanding cop, she can be very trusting of her guys, even after Kelly Jo's death. She hands that key out whenever it's asked for, only requiring the officer to sign the sheet she has for that purpose. In time and out time included."

Clara stood and paced behind the desk. "So, someone signs out the key, makes a copy, returns the regular key, and uses the duplicate whenever they need to get in here to delete the files. But why these files? They're old, almost as old as the precinct. What could they be hiding?"

Morgan looked her straight in the eyes. "That's what you're going to find out, Ms. Young. Isn't that why you're really here?"

Clara paled. "I, um, well, I'm just the intern. I'm here to help."

He shook his head. "You're not a very good liar. And while you worked very enthusiastically yesterday on all those files, you definitely were only half paying attention to what you were doing. You were also observing everything that went on in this room—who came in, who checked out what, that sort of thing."

Clara raised one eyebrow. "And you were observing me?"

"I'm a cop, Ms. Young. It's what I do."

"And what did you decide, Mr. Morgan?"

He placed his hands on his hips. "I've decided that you have a knack for solving mysteries. And that the captain decided to do you a solid and let you intern here, giving you police experience while also giving you the ability to try to figure out this murder, since no one else has been able to."

Clara stopped pacing. She stood in front of him, her stance matching his. Today, Morgan wore a blue striped tie and a white button-up shirt. Her eyes kept falling to the tie, its colors mesmerizing. "That's actually very correct, Mr. Morgan. I'm just here to help. I'm not going to step on any toes. I just want to find out what happened to Kelly Jo." Clara looked back at the computer. "I thought the files would be the best place to start. I was going to go through the ones that Kelly Jo had entered herself, but those are gone too."

He held up a finger. "Not necessarily." Morgan reached into his pocket and pulled out a USB drive. "After you left last night, I saved everything you did. You spent so much time working on it, I hated to think that it was just going to get erased." He handed her the USB and smiled. "Kelly Jo's stuff should be on there, too. For whatever reason, the mole never deleted her stuff until today."

Clara looked down at the USB in her hand. "Maybe because before yesterday, the mole never thought anyone would look at the stuff Kelly Jo had already entered. But now that I'm here, they're worried that I'll do just that." She grinned. "Ready to see what they don't want us to see?"

He nodded and stepped up behind her as she sat back down, plugging in the USB as she did.

Several clicks later, Clara was looking at her filled-out spreadsheet. Everything was where she had entered it the day before. Clicking to the front page, she found the entries made by

Kelly Jo, right where they had been the day before. Grinning, she looked up at Morgan. "Thank goodness. I think today I want to look at the evidence that Kelly Jo was cataloging. It wasn't this box, was it?"

He shook his head. "No, Kelly Jo had started on newer stuff, thinking that it was more important, since the cases were still being tried." He turned to the cage and pulled the key ring out of his pocket. "I'll grab that box for you."

Clara sat back and looked at the spreadsheet. Morgan had let her work all day yesterday on something that Kelly Jo had never touched, had let her leave knowing that her files would probably disappear overnight, and hadn't said anything. But he had saved her files, just in case. Meaning he did know a thing or two about the computer, whether he wanted to admit it or not. Clara turned as he walked out of the cage, box in hand. It had significantly less dust on it than the other box had. A lot less wear as well. He set it down in front of her and stepped back. "Morgan, why did you give me the old box yesterday? Were you testing me?"

He nodded. "Yes, I was. I had to see if you were truly serious about this, about what Kelly Jo was doing. It was only after you spent almost all afternoon so lost in that box that I realized you must be here for other reasons besides cataloging. I looked up your dad. A sheriff's daughter, cataloging evidence? It didn't take long to figure that one out."

Clara looked down at the box, placing a hand on the cover. "I have to figure out what happened to her. I will figure out what happened to her." She looked up at Morgan, expecting him to laugh in her face. She wasn't even a cop. What could she possibly do that they hadn't already done?

Instead, she met that steely gaze, the one that he had directed at her when she had walked through the door the day before. "Something tells me that you will. You need anything, you let me know." With that, he sat down at his desk and opened up his crossword book.

Clara turned to the evidence box and slowly opened it. This was what Kelly Jo had been working on. This could be the key to figuring out why she had been murdered. Clara was excited to get started.

Lunch approached much faster than she anticipated. Will actually came to the evidence room, poking his head through the unlocked door with a smile. "Anyone hungry in here?"

Morgan grunted and looked at his watch. "Almost that time. Harry and Ralph will be by soon to eat with me. You should take Ms. Young to get something to eat. She's been in that seat all morning." When Clara stood up, stretching her arms over her head, she gave Morgan a questioning look. She wanted to see if Will would know anything about a mole in the precinct, but Morgan shook his head slightly. Clara took that to mean she shouldn't share anything and she gave a nod of her own. Will didn't seem to notice this exchange.

He held the door open for her as she headed out.

"So, how's the cataloging going?" The question sounded harmless enough, but now Clara wondered if it truly was. Could she trust him?

She decided to keep her answers as neutral as possible. "It's going. It's a very slow and tedious job. And wouldn't you believe it, all my entries had been erased when I got in this morning." This was a test, not for Will, but for anyone in earshot. The mole would know that the files had been deleted. If Clara didn't mention it at least once, that would seem sketchy. She didn't have to say anything about the fact that Morgan had backed them up.

Will's brow crinkled and his eyes flashed. "Erased? All of them?"

Clara nodded. "Even Kelly Jo's entries were gone, which is super weird because the box I was working on yesterday didn't have anything to do with the one she had been working on."

Will seemed to think about this for a moment. "Maybe it was a computer glitch. Like a hard drive problem or something. One of the tech guys could take a look if you asked."

Clara nodded, pretending to consider the suggestion. "Good idea. Point me in their direction after lunch, OK?"

Will agreed and walked her out to the taco truck, where a line had already formed. Alice stood there among the other officers, watching as they approached. She smiled up at Will, her whole face brightening. Instantly, Clara realized what was going on, though Will seemed oblivious. Suddenly, Alice's abrasive behavior made sense. She had a crush on Will and felt threatened by the attention he was giving Clara. Clara stepped forward and stood within Alice's earshot. She turned to Will with a smile. "So my boyfriend works all this weekend, but maybe one day next week we could all get together for dinner. Do you have a girlfriend?"

It was such a change in topic that Will stopped, his whole body freezing. His hands came up in front of him, like he was trying to physically block the question. Clara saw this but wasn't really paying attention to him. Her attention was on Alice, who had visibly relaxed the minute Clara had mentioned having a boyfriend.

Clara grinned, glad her plan had worked. Looking up at Will, she saw that he still hadn't moved. "Uh, Will? Are you OK?"

He dropped his hands and put them behind his back. His head dropped. "I, uh, don't have a girlfriend." His voice was so low, Clara almost didn't hear it.

She patted his shoulder, trying to catch his eyes. "It's OK. I'm pretty sure I can help with that. Why not just bring a friend from the precinct?"

"Wouldn't that be weird?"

"How so? It's just dinner. It's not like I'm expecting you to pick your future wife. Why don't I pick someone for you to bring?"

He motioned to the line. "There's your options. Mostly male. Not exactly to my taste."

Clara nodded, trying to keep a serious look on her face. "Yes, the pool to draw from is small, but not empty. What about Alice? I bet she'd love a night out with a good meal."

At the mention of her name, Alice whipped her head toward Clara. Will didn't seem to notice, as he gave Clara the most frightened look she'd ever seen. "Alice?" He gulped. "Do you really think she would agree to go to dinner with us?"

Clara planted her hands on her hips, all seriousness gone. "Now, Will, are you telling me that you're afraid to ask Alice to dinner? She won't bite."

Will sighed. "But she could say no. They usually do."

The line moved a foot and Clara took another step closer to the truck. "What do you mean?"

When he looked into her eyes, Clara saw pain and anguish. "If you haven't noticed, I'm not exactly the most handsome guy around. All through high school, most girls turned me down. Or made me their best friend so that it was super awkward to ask them out."

Clara bit her lip. "Like I did. You came up to me and were super nice and I immediately put you in the friend zone."

He shook his head. "No, it's OK. I didn't eat lunch with you yesterday because I wanted to ask you out. I did it because you seemed lonely and I wanted you to feel welcome. But the conversation today kind of reminded me of all those other times."

They had reached the window of the taco truck and they ordered. Clara got the same thing from the day before. Then they headed over to the tree, where Will set down the towel he had brought with him. Clara sat and leaned against the tree, watching the other officers get their tacos. She looked at Will, who seemed rather down after their talk. "Will, the only reason I suggested you ask Alice is that I think she likes you."

Will choked, lettuce spewing from his mouth. He grabbed a napkin and wiped at his chin. "Uh, what?"

Clara smiled. "I think she likes you. She was very short with me yesterday, but that I expected, since she wasn't expecting me. This morning, I thought it would be better, that I'd at least get a smile out of her. But no, I came walking in with you and she shot darts at my head with her eyes. Then, in line, she watched as you walked up. She was super tense until I mentioned that I had a boyfriend. Will, the way she visibly relaxed after I said that? She has a thing for you and feels threatened by me."

He took another bite of taco, his eyebrows scrunched up in concentration. "Do you really think so?"

Clara nodded. "Will, I'm almost positive that she likes you. Why not ask her? If she says no, then she says no. But if you never ask, you'll never know. You could miss out on a great opportunity."

Clara finished her first taco and started on the second while Will contemplated what to do. He looked over to where Alice sat on a bench with two other female officers, their heads close together in discussion as they ate. He looked back at Clara. "When should I ask her?"

Clara looked over at Alice's group. "Not around her friends. It's always awkward getting asked out in front of your friends. Wait until after lunch, when she's back at the front desk. Ask her there, when she's alone."

He brushed the last of the lettuce off his top and straightened his shoulders. "And you really think she'll say yes?"

Clara laughed. "I do. And if she does, you'd better come tell me. We can work out the plans for dinner once you've secured her yes."

Clara walked back to the evidence room a little bit lighter. The fact that Will had seemed so surprised that Alice liked him, and then so nervous to ask her out, had been sweet. She sat back down in front of the computer, determined to retrace Kelly Jo's steps as far as possible. It would be a good distraction until Will showed up with his news.

7.

DINNER FOR FOUR

Clara didn't hear the door open when Will finally came back with Alice's answer. She had managed to make it only a fourth of the way through the box—nowhere near what Kelly Jo had achieved—and she was feeling discouraged. Everything Kelly Jo had entered was still in the box. Nothing seemed to be missing, and Clara was starting to feel like she was on a wild goose chase. If the reason Kelly Jo died was in this box, Clara wasn't sure she'd figure it out.

Will cleared his throat, bringing her out of her gloomy thoughts. She looked up and smiled. "Well?"

Will's face broke out into a grin. "She said yes. To dinner." He bent down next to Clare and took her hands in his. "How did you know?"

"Will, you're a cop. Don't you pay attention to body language?"

He shook his head. "I've never been very good at that. I always misread it. Or I don't see it. Sometimes it feels like I'm just looking in the wrong direction."

Clara rolled her eyes. "Oh, man. Such a guy. Look, if a girl likes you, she gives very clear signals with her body. Leaning in close, showing you her chest, staring at you with her eyes."

His lips parted and he looked into her eyes. "Like you are now?"

Clara blinked and pulled back from him. "Exactly, just like that. I was giving you an example." She tucked her hair behind her ears and turned back to the computer. "So, I was thinking dinner at my apartment, Monday night? I'll cook, you bring the drinks."

He stood up and rubbed his hands on his pants. "Sounds good to me. 7 p.m.?"

Clara smiled up at him. "Perfect."

Will headed to the door and turned back, still smiling. "Have a good weekend. See you Monday."

As the door shut behind him, Morgan turned to her. "Playing matchmaker?"

Clara shrugged and reached for another file. "She likes him, he seems to like her. What's wrong with giving them a little push?"

Morgan stood, gathering his things. "Nothing, except that when it falls apart you'll have to pick up the pieces."

Clara set down the file and turned to him. "And who says it will fall apart?" Morgan remained silent, watching her. "Is it because they're cops? Because they work in the same precinct? Look, it can be tough, and a heck of a lot of work, but if they end up really caring for each other, what does it matter?"

Morgan held up his hands in mock surrender. "I'm just saying, you don't know Alice's history. There's a reason she has front desk duty and it's not because she's a girl." He headed toward the door. "You just need to be careful about who you set her up with." He paused at the door and looked at his watch. "Also, it's time to call it a day. Let's get this stuff put away." Morgan set his stuff back down at his desk and took the box back into the cage. Meanwhile, Clara saved everything she had done on the USB drive, then shut down the computer. She wanted to ask Morgan what he meant about Alice but she wasn't sure where to start. Or that he would even tell her what he was talking about.

Before he made it to the door, she gave it a shot. "So, Alice goes through men like wildfire? Or she just steals their money and breaks their hearts?"

He turned to look at her. "She got her partner killed. They were patrolling, heard gunfire, went in to respond, and when they did, all hell broke loose. She forgot to call for backup, which left them pinned in an area where they couldn't escape, trading shots with the bad guys. Her partner had been shot in the initial altercation and when she finally called it in, you know, like we're trained to do, it was too late. He died before the ambulance ever made it to them. If she had followed protocol, called for backup when she should have, and called in his gunshot immediately, he'd still be alive."

Morgan's whole body was shaking. For the first time, she saw the steely calm of his eyes change to anger. "He was a friend." She said it as a statement, not a question.

"A very good one. And a damn fine cop. He relied on his partner to do her job and she failed him. No one will work with her, no one will partner up with her, but she won't leave. So the captain put her on desk duty. It was either that or stick her in here and I wouldn't tolerate that." He stomped out of the room and locked the door as he went, leaving Clara to scramble after him in silence.

All the way home, Clara doubted her decision to set up Will with Alice. Was Morgan right? Was Alice dangerous? She had made a mistake on the job, a fatal mistake. But the job and her personal life weren't one and the same. The fact that her partner had died shouldn't affect her ability to find someone. Did Will know about the accident? And if he did, was that why he was hesitant to ask Alice out?

Clara called Hannah as she walked through her door. Hannah picked up on the first ring, munching on something crunchy. "What's up, girl?"

Clara sighed. "I may have stuck my nose where it doesn't belong." Clara could hear Hannah adjusting her position on the other end of the phone. With long legs and dark black hair, Hannah was the epitome of grace. She was also the daughter of a policeman, so a good person to bounce things off of.

"What did you do?"

"I set up a cop with another cop, not knowing that the girl cop is kind of off-limits."

"Off-limits? Like, she's married or something?"

"I wish. No, she got her partner killed by not following protocol. She's pulling front desk duty. And now I'm not sure if I should've set them up in the first place."

Hannah chuckled. "Well, why did you think it was a good idea originally?"

"She didn't like me. And I figured out it was because this guy was paying attention to me. So, I thought if I got them to double date with me and Anthony, maybe he would like her the way she apparently likes him."

"But let me guess. The other cops aren't too keen on this idea. She can't be trusted, that sort of thing." Not waiting for a response, Hannah plowed ahead. "Clara, you know how cops are. They're stubborn. If this guy is young, he may not see her the way the others do. He may like her as much as she likes him."

"But the cop I talked to today told me I'd have to pick up the pieces. Do they really think she'd hurt him?"

"It's a protective thing. Cops are like that. You know this. Don't sweat it. If it doesn't work out, at least you tried." More munching. "So, besides playing matchmaker, what have you been up to? I heard you got an internship at the local precinct."

Clara fidgeted with the engagement ring on her finger, grinning. "I did. How else do you think I met cops?"

Hannah's laugh filled Clara with joy. "But Clara, I know you. There's something more to this. Spill." More munching awaited her response.

"There was a murder a couple years back. A girl, not much older than us. Top of her class, real smart, you know the type. Found stabbed to death in the evidence room, in the one blind spot provided by the cameras. They haven't been able to solve it."

Hannah's sigh worried Clara. "And you think you can?" The small hint of doubt in her voice made Clara deflate.

"Well, I mean, it can't hurt to look, right? Interns don't get noticed, Hannah. People are more likely to say things around me than they would around other cops. She was working in Evidence, so that's where I'm working, following in her footsteps."

"What was she doing in Evidence?"

"Helping convert all their hard-copy files to digital. It's a long process, with lots of spreadsheets. And there's a mole."

The munching stopped. "What do you mean there's a mole?"

Clara flung herself on her couch and threw an arm over her head. "The first day, I spent cataloging a box of really old files, like 50 years old." Hannah snorted. "OK, old to me. Anyway, come in the next morning and all the files are gone. And when I say gone, I mean erased. There was nothing. Everything, even the stuff that had been entered by the girl before me, was gone."

"Computer glitch?"

"I thought so, but the cop who runs Evidence said that has happened to him every time he tries to input anything into the computer. Well, not that exactly. He said it was the first time her stuff had disappeared, too. What he didn't tell me was that the night before, he saved all my work to a USB drive. So, really, I didn't lose anything. But whoever deleted it thinks I did."

"So, they're hiding something. Maybe that something is what got her killed?"

Clara sat up. "That's exactly what I was thinking. If I find it, I may find out who did it. It's worth a shot. What else am I going to do?"

Clara wanted to take back the words as soon as she said them. They tasted bitter in her mouth. Hannah paused before responding. "You aren't happy there, are you?"

Tears threatened to prevent Clara from talking. "I'm just lonely. I'm not in classes yet, so no new friends. Anthony is always so busy with the frat that I don't see him as often as I thought I would. I thought about getting a job but he won't let me, saying that once school starts I wouldn't be able to keep it. But he has a job. That's how I'm living in this apartment."

"Does the internship pay anything?"

Clara bit her lip. "It does. Not much, minimum wage, but it's something. Don't tell Anthony. He thinks this is all for school even though I've told him about Kelly Jo."

Hannah snorted. "Girl, I don't even talk to Anthony. I would never tell him. You do what you gotta do. If you feel you need to solve this girl's murder, then go for it. I'm going to worry like crazy about you but I know you can take care of yourself." She paused. "Although, maybe take self-defense classes? Like martial arts or something."

Clara laughed, relaxing. "I really should. Imagine what I could've done to Andrew if I had."

They dissolved into giggles, talking about Clara being a super ninja and taking out bad guys. Hannah had to beg off shortly after, though she promised to call Clara later.

Clara stumbled into the kitchen, hungry but not really sure what she wanted to eat. She popped a frozen dinner into the microwave, not even paying attention to what it was. She was halfway through it when her phone rang. Glancing at the number, she smiled. "Hey."

Stacy heaved a huge sigh on the other end of the line. "Oh, thank goodness. I was worried you wouldn't answer. OK, fill me in about this internship. I'm all ears."

As Clara recapped what she was doing and why she was doing it, she felt lucky to have such great friends. Even from far away, they thought about each other and encouraged each other.

Once she finished, Stacy's only response made Clara laugh. "Well, what's taking you so long? Come on, super sleuth, find this killer already!" After a slight pause, she got more serious. "But really, I mean it. If anyone can figure this out, it's you."

Clara stretched her arms over her head, the phone pressed between her shoulder and her ear. "I sure hope so. No one deserves to have their murder go unsolved."

Stacy agreed. Then she wished Clara good luck and goodnight. Clara fell into bed, her heart full of the love and support of her friends. She tried to think about what she should do with Will and Alice come Monday.

***

That weekend, Clara surprised Anthony at work. Knowing that he didn't like to eat the food at the places where he worked, she brought him a packed lunch and waited until his break to eat it with him. Fixing egg salad sandwiches and bringing grapes for him to enjoy was the easy part. Finding the nerve to tell him about the double date would be the hard part. It took most of his break for her to finally figure out what to say. Finally, she decided to just blurt it out. "So, we're having people over at the apartment tomorrow night."

Anthony stopped mid-bite and looked at her. "'We'?"

She gave him her best smile. "Yes, 'we.' I may have played matchmaker at the precinct yesterday. The cop at the front desk doesn't seem to like me. And I kind of figure it's because the guy she likes has been eating lunch with me." Anthony stiffened at this. Clara patted his knee. "So I suggested that we do a double date with them, at the apartment. He has never asked her out because he assumed she would say no. Apparently, he got told no a lot when he was younger."

"And you think them going on a double date with us is going to kick start their relationship?"

Clara shrugged. "It provides a safe environment. They can go as just friends and test the waters, no expectations." She looked down at her hands, which were fiddling with the hem of her shirt.

He smiled. "Sounds like it's going to be fun, babe. What're we eating?"

Clara relaxed, the tension in her shoulders easing. "I was thinking pot roast, in the Crockpot. It could cook all day and be ready when we got home."

His smile grew bigger. "I love pot roast."

Clara laughed. The sound rang around the room. "I know. I'm doing that on purpose. To ensure you come."

He took her hand. "Why would I not come?"

Clara bit her lip. She didn't want to ruin the moment, so she kept most of her feelings to herself. "Well, if the frat ends up doing something, I just wanted to ensure that you picked me over them."

Anthony pressed his head against hers. "I will always pick you." He kissed her, then stood and pulled her to her feet. "Duty calls. Tomorrow night? What time?"

"Seven p.m. Get there early if you can. That way, you can help me get everything ready." He nodded, gave her another kiss, then headed out of the break room and back to the main floor. Clara watched him go and bit her lip. While she had no doubt that he believed he would choose her over the frat, she wasn't so sure that it would end up like that. It felt like she was losing him and she didn't know how to stop it.

***

The next evening, Clara walked into the apartment to a smell that made her think of home. As the pot roast overwhelmed her senses, she inhaled deeply. She headed into the kitchen, grabbed plates, and started setting the

103

table for four. Clara looked at the clock over her sink and saw that she had about 45 minutes before Will and Alice would be there. She pulled out her phone and shot Anthony a text, reminding him to grab dessert on his way over. She received a smiley face in response and sighed, happy to know that he still intended to come.

Ten minutes before they were to arrive, Anthony charged through the door, two pies in hand. "They had key lime and lemon meringue, so I got both." He set them down on the counter and took a huge breath. "Man, that smells good." He headed over to the Crockpot and lifted the lid for another sniff. Then he grabbed the fork off the counter, snatched out a carrot, and popped it into his mouth. His moan seemed to go on forever. "That's so good." He stepped over to Clara and kissed her cheek. "You're amazing."

Clara giggled, rolling her eyes. "No more stealing. Help me get it spooned out and on the table." Anthony did as directed, spooning out each component and bringing the bowls to the table. He saved the meat for last. It fell apart as he took it out of the Crockpot. Clara smiled over his shoulder. "Perfection."

As he set the meat on the table, Anthony said, "So, tell me about this guy. You said he eats lunch with you?"

Clara nodded. She took off her apron and pulled her hair out of its ponytail. "Yeah. I had planned to eat by myself, but that first day he sat next to me in the grass and talked to me. It was nice since I hadn't really had a very warm welcome from anyone else."

"Like this girl you had him ask out?"

"Exactly. She glares at me. Today was better, though. She still didn't smile, but she also didn't glare. I guess that's better than nothing."

Anthony rubbed the back of his neck. "You sure you want to do this? It might end up being awkward."

Clara shrugged. "I just don't want her to feel threatened. I'm not after him. Not even interested in him." She wrapped her arms around Anthony's neck and pulled him close. His warm breath on her cheek sent tingles down her spine. "I already have a man." As they leaned in for a kiss, a knock sounded at the door. Clara pulled away, sighing. Anthony winked at her and headed to the door.

Will stood on the other side, Alice on his arm. Both looked nervous. Will's free hand strayed up to his hair as he walked in. Alice couldn't stop fidgeting with her shirt, while her eyes darted all over the room. Clara grabbed their free hands and pulled them farther inside. "Welcome to my humble apartment. Dinner is ready!"

Once they had all been seated, Clara offered them sweet tea. Both accepted, holding out their glasses. Will drank so much of his, Clara had to pour him another glass. She sat between Anthony and Alice, smiling at Alice as she did. "Help yourselves. Dig right in."

Will and Anthony started filling their plates, but Alice sat, watching. Clara leaned toward her. "Aren't you hungry?"

Alice looked at Clara and narrowed her dark brown eyes. "I am. I'll just wait for the boys to get their fill first." She'd worn her blonde hair down and the ends were curled. Her flowing green shirt and cropped skirt looked more relaxed than Clara had expected. This close to her, Clara could see that Alice had a small spattering of freckles across the bridge of her nose.

As soon as the boys had filled their plates, Alice dug in. Clara did as well, watching Alice from the corner of her eye. She took more potatoes than anything else, covering them in salt. Clara cringed, imagining how that would feel in her mouth. All conversation died as the food was consumed. The only sounds were those of forks scratching against plates.

Once the meal was over, Clara invited them to move to the couch while she and Anthony cleaned up. He washed

107

while she rinsed and dried, then placed the dishes back where they belonged. Will offered to help but Clara shooed him back to the couch, telling him that he was a guest and to entertain Alice. Clara strained to hear what they said as she and Anthony cleaned. Anthony leaned in, his mouth close to her ear. "He's very awkward."

Clara nodded. "I noticed. But she's not helping. She's hardly speaking to him."

Anthony looked over his shoulder. "She's leaning into him, but it's like she expects him to do all the work. Poor guy doesn't know what he's supposed to do in the first place."

"Maybe a game will liven things up? Like Phase Ten?"

He laughed. "You just want a rematch."

She nudged him with her elbow. "You know it. And you know I'll win this time."

As soon as they finished, Clara went into her bedroom to grab the cards. When she came back out, Alice had scooted closer to Will, but only because Anthony had claimed the third cushion on the couch. Anthony reached over to the coffee table and pulled off the magazines stacked on it. He set them next to the couch. Under her arm, Clara had tucked a pillow from her bed. She set it on the floor, on the opposite side of the coffee table. "OK, who's up for a game of Phase Ten?"

Will's face lit up and he leaned forward with his elbows on his knees. "I'm pretty good at this, you know."

Anthony leaned around Alice. "So is Clara. You better watch out."

Will laughed, his whole body shaking. Alice seemed to shrink between the two men, looking from one to the other uncertainly.

"Um, I don't know how to play."

From her spot on the floor, Clara stopped shuffling and looked up at Alice.

She could see that Alice's lip was quivering. "Oh, Alice, you'll love it. It's so much fun. Here, I'll explain the rules." As she shuffled, Clara went over the different phases and what one had to do to complete each one. She explained the different cards, the colors, and the numbers, including the points for each card. Alice seemed to be interested, as she nodded at all of Clara's instructions.

Once the game got into full swing, everyone settled down. Will and Alice relaxed around each other. The tension left their shoulders and laughter came easy to them now. Anthony ended up on the floor next to Clara, half the time pretending to look at her cards. As usual, she pulled ahead, but Alice had turned out to be a quick study and was able to keep up with her. When Alice came out with the winning hand and ended the game, Clara fell back in defeat. "Beaten. How could I be beaten?"

Anthony laughed, tossing his cards in that air. "Finally, the queen has been conquered."

Will stood up and pulled Alice with him, flinging her around in a circle. "And you didn't even know how to play!"

Alice laughed. "Actually, I did." All eyes turned to her.

"But you had me explain the entire game," Clara said.

Alice nodded. "Of course I did. So I could gauge how you played. I watched you the whole time you talked about those cards. I watched your facial expressions. That way, I had some idea of what was in your hand each time." She shrugged. "Pretty easy way to play."

Anthony's mouth slammed closed with a click. His eyes widened. Will took a step back from Alice and shoved his hands in his pockets. Clara could see the doubt on his face, the worry making his eyebrows meet in the middle of his forehead. Alice didn't seem to notice their reactions. She was oblivious to having done or said anything strange. Clara had no idea how to save the evening. Looking at the clock and seeing how late it was, she decided that she didn't have to. She had given Alice a shot. If Alice blew it, that was her own fault.

Rubbing her hands together, Clara tried to smile. "I guess that comes with being a cop, huh?" When Alice only looked at her in confusion, Clara coughed. "It's getting pretty late. I think it's time to call it a night."

Anthony stretched and yawned in mock exhaustion. "I agree. Really should be getting back to the house." He looked at Will and Alice. "I'll walk you two out." Clara walked them to the door. Anthony kissed her before he headed out. His eyes conveyed more than what he could say out loud. Alice's words still rang in her ears.

After picking up the cards and heading into her room, Clara pulled out her journal. "Alice is throwing me off. I really think she likes Will, but the way she acted tonight, it was almost like she was expecting him to bend over backward for her. Then her response to winning at Phase Ten … it was very calculated. Maybe everything she does is calculated." Again, Clara stashed the journal back in her drawer. Then, after slipping off her pants and shirt, she climbed under her covers. As she closed her eyes, Clara couldn't get Alice's words out of her head. What person played a game that way?

8.

A CLUE IN THE BOX

The next day, Clara felt the tension at work. Alice didn't even look her way when she walked through the door, and she didn't see Will on her way up to the evidence room. When Clara opened the door, Morgan was waiting for her, his arms crossed. He watched silently as she sat down at her desk and booted up the computer. He waited until she was reaching for the box before saying, "Didn't go so well, did it?"

Clara looked over at him. "Alice is, um, strange."

Morgan nodded. "Told you."

Clara gripped the desk, her nails biting into the wood. "No, you really didn't. You told me about one incident that ended with her at the front desk. You never mentioned any personality issues."

"I didn't think I had to after that story."

Clara sighed and rubbed her temples. "Look, I don't know what you were trying to convey with the story, but it didn't get through, OK? We did the double date. It was weird. I don't think we'll be doing it again."

"And Will?"

"What about Will? I haven't seen him yet."

"Exactly." Morgan went back to his desk and picked up his crossword puzzle.

Clara pulled the box toward her, dust flying in her face. Trying to keep from coughing, she opened it and pulled out the next file. Morgan could be mad at her all he wanted. She had a job to do.

Clara spent the next several hours working through the box, pulling file after file out of it. This particular box held files pertaining to a kidnapping case that had taken place in the 1980s. Right before lunch, Clara reached into the box, only to pull out something that was definitely not a file. She stared at it for a full minute before clearing her throat. "Um, Morgan, I think you need to see this."

He grunted, not looking up from his crossword book.

"No, I mean, really. Look up."

When his eyes moved toward her, he almost fell out of his chair. Clara clutched a knife, dried blood crusted on its serrated blade.

Her hand trembled as she looked at him. "What do I do?"

"We never found a murder weapon." He stood and pulled an evidence bag from a drawer in his desk. "Everyone assumed the killer took it with them."

"You're telling me that after she died, no one went through these boxes?" Clara dropped the knife into the bag and looked at her hand like it had been contaminated.

Morgan shook his head while sealing the bag. "Nothing had been disturbed. This box was still on her desk when we found her. She was inside the cage, around the corner in the blind spot, nowhere near the box." He shrugged. "We figured it wasn't the box the killer was interested in, but her."

He set the bag with the knife on his desk and reached for his phone. "I'm calling the captain down here."

Clara nodded and sat back down in her chair to wait.

It didn't take the captain long to get to them. She burst through the door and swept into the room. "Where is it?"

Morgan held up the bag for her. She took it and turned the knife over in her hands.

"It was right here the whole time. And we missed it."

"The killer made us miss it," Morgan said. "This isn't our fault."

The captain glared at him, like she could burn him with her eyes. "Not our fault? A young girl died here, in a building full of cops, and we haven't been able to figure out who did it. All because we don't want to point the finger at each other." She slammed the knife down on his desk. "I want every test run on this. I want to know where it was made, how many owners it had, who bought it. I want to know everything." She stormed out of the room, taking what felt like most of the air with her.

Clara let out a breath, a slow whistle leaving her lips. "Is that even possible?"

He shook his head. "Not really. We can find out make and model. But where it was sold? Who bought it? Wishful thinking." He rubbed his face with one big hand. "It's lunchtime. Go get some fresh air."

Clara headed out but stopped at the door. "Morgan, I really didn't mean to get Will hurt."

He looked at her, sadness clouding his steely gaze. "And I didn't mean for Kelly Jo to die. We all make mistakes." He turned his back to her, giving her no chance to continue the conversation.

At the taco truck, Alice marched up to Clara. "He's avoiding me."

Clara took a step back, unsure of what to say. She looked around, but Will was nowhere to be seen. "If it helps, he's avoiding me too," Clara said.

Alice's shoulders sagged, the tension leaving them. "So it's not just me?"

Clara shook her head. "No, I think he just needs space. Let's get some food and leave him be." They stood in line together, but when it came time to sit down, Clara went back to her tree alone, clutching her food to her chest. It was like the first day all over again, though with no Will and no towel to take her mind off things.

Leaning with her back against the tree, she sighed and unwrapped her

119

tacos. As she took her first bite, she heard a voice behind her ask, "Are you alone?"

Clara turned her head one way, then the other. "Will? Where are you?"

"Don't turn around. Hold your taco in front of your mouth." Clara did as instructed. "I'm behind the tree."

"But why?"

She heard him adjust his position. "I don't know. Embarrassed?"

"But you didn't do anything wrong. You weren't the awkward one." Clara took a bite of her taco, thinking over her words carefully. "Will, I'm sorry."

"It wasn't your fault."

"But it was. I suggested it. I pointed out the way she was eyeing you. If I hadn't said anything, you wouldn't have asked her out." Clara groaned.

"Clara, I wouldn't have asked her out if I wasn't interested in her too. I just didn't know if she would say yes. You gave me the confidence to believe that she would."

"And then it totally fell apart. I don't even know how to address what she said."

"You're telling me. She manipulated you into giving away your tells by explaining the game to her. Who does that?"

"A really good cop?"

He snorted, the sound bringing a smile to Clara's lips. "No way. Not even Morgan does that. And he's the best cop I know."

"Wait, what? Morgan? As in my Morgan?"

"I mean, if that's what we're labeling him as now, sure. Your Morgan, the one you spend every day with. He's a great poker player but he doesn't manipulate people."

Clara stored away that piece of information for later examination. "Back to Alice. She seems pretty upset, if that makes it any better. But I don't think she realizes what she did that was so strange." Clara leaned around the tree so she could see him.

Will turned his pale face toward her. Bags sat under his grey eyes. "I just don't feel comfortable going out with her again. How do I tell her that?"

"Be honest with her. No one likes to be lied to. And if she's as good at reading people as she seems, she'll be able to tell if you lie to her."

He nodded and pushed himself off the ground. "Dating is hard."

Clara smiled up at him. "Once you get done talking to her, I have news you might be interested in." He raised his eyebrows, but Clara pointed to where Alice was sitting, eating lunch by herself.

Will trudged toward her, head down, shoulders slumped, like a man walking to his death. From where she sat, Clara couldn't hear them, but their body language told her all she needed to know. Alice stiffened. Her eyes flitted to Clara and then back to Will's face. Clara shoved what was left of her taco into her mouth, unable to take her eyes off them. Will's hands were flying around, gesturing between himself and Alice. Alice nodded, but she didn't seem as accepting of what he was saying as Clara thought she would be. Instead of smiling, Alice seemed to fold into herself, getting smaller, if that was even possible. Will turned back to Clara, shot her a thumbs up, and headed over to the taco truck. Clara looked up to find Alice starring at her, her gaze unwavering. Clara gathered her things and headed back inside, keeping her eyes on the ground.

Morgan was waiting for her in the evidence room, his arms folded. "Well?"

"Well, he was honest with her. She still hates me but at least she'll leave him alone."

Morgan nodded, then went back to his crossword. Clara tapped her pencil on the desk and looked at the box. "What do you think they'll find on the knife?"

He looked up at her. "Nothing. This killer was smart. They knew to hide the knife in the box, as walking out of the precinct with it wouldn't be an option."

"How did it get in here in the first place?"

Morgan leaned forward, hands on his knees, his crossword abandoned. "I went through some of Kelly Jo's notes while you were at lunch. That knife was logged as evidence in another case. That's how it ended up here."

"Maybe that case is the one that got her killed?"

He shook his head. "No, definitely not."

"But what if she found something related to that case and the killer used the knife because it would get rid of evidence by covering it in Kelly Jo's blood and-"

He held up a hand, waiting for her silence. "It's not that case. I worked that case."

"You?"

He nodded. "It was my last case. The one I got injured on." He rubbed his leg, an unconscious habit Clara had seen him repeat multiple times a day. "I'm the one who bagged that knife. Do you think I killed Kelly Jo?"

Clara shook her head. "No way. You don't strike me as the dirty-cop kind of person. I have this feeling you do everything by the book."

For the first time since she had started working with him, Morgan smiled. His whole face moved with the action. "You've got that right."

Clara giggled, then clapped her hand over her mouth. "I'm sorry, but that was just too perfect." She took a deep breath. "OK, so it wasn't you. The knife was just convenient. But it was at the bottom of the box and I didn't find anything amiss in the files that I've gone through so far."

He looked back at the cage. "It must still be in there."

Clara rubbed her face. "You think so? You think it's still in there? Why would the killer leave it in there?"

"Not enough time. Kelly Jo was killed during lunch, while I was out of the room and all the cops were getting food at the taco truck. Meaning, everyone was out front, eating. And there wasn't enough time to get whatever it was they didn't want Kelly Jo to see and take it out. So, it's still in here somewhere." Morgan turned back to Clara, his steely gaze boring into her.

"Then I'll find it. Next box, please." Into the box, Clara placed all the files that had already been entered. She then replaced the top and set the box on the floor. Morgan picked it up and carried it back to the cage. The box he brought out was the one on which she had started the first day.

She looked up at him, her brows wrinkling. He placed a hand on the box, causing dust to flutter up. "I know you want to find out who killed Kelly Jo but you were brought in here to do a job and I think maybe it would keep suspicion off you if you at least do part of it." He took the top off the box and set it on the floor. "It may not seem important to you, but it is to me."

Clara nodded and pulled out the top file. She had already gotten halfway through the box before she switched boxes, so there wasn't as much left in this one. "I get it. I have a job to do." She stopped and looked up at Morgan. "Kelly Jo died during lunch? Is that why I've never been left alone in here?"

His eyes went from hard to soft in an instant. "I made that mistake once. I will never make it again."

A thought suddenly occurred to Clara, one that made her pause. "And Will? Did he seek me out because you asked him to?" At Morgan's slow nod, Clara's head dipped. "Today, he said you were the best cop he knew. It makes sense that he'd do whatever you asked him to do." She opened the file, sadness creeping over her. Will hadn't even wanted to befriend her.

"Don't let that make you think he didn't want to." Clara's head snapped up and her mouth hung open. Another smile had spread across Morgan's face. "He's a sweet kid and probably would've gone out of his way to be nice to you anyway. But I needed it to happen faster than Will's normal pace, which is slow and steady. So, I asked him to do me a favor, befriend you, keep an eye on you, protect you if necessary."

Clara took a deep breath. "That's comforting to know."

He went back to his seat, still smiling at her. "He came to you today, right? After the embarrassing incident at your apartment?"

"Yeah, he did."

"He trusts you. He's not hanging around you just because I asked him to. He sees you as a friend. Does it matter how that friendship started?"

Clara shook her head, a small smile appearing on her lips. "No, you're right. It just threw me for a loop." She went back to the file. Clara typed in the case number before she went through the evidence list. The way Kelly Jo had set up the system, Clara had to verify that each piece of evidence was still in the box with its corresponding case number. Clara looked over at Morgan. "Do you think something is missing? I mean, why else would Kelly Jo be killed? Unless she was going to uncover the fact that evidence had been tampered with or stolen altogether."

He nodded. "It's a good possibility, but we won't know until you find it." At that moment, an officer walked in, evidence bags in hand. While Morgan got busy checking them in, Clara went back to the files, curious about what she would find and when she would find it. There was no doubt in her mind that there was something to find. Why else would Kelly Jo have been killed?

9.

SUSPICIOUS ACTIVITY

Clara spent most of the next week cataloging box after box after box. She ate lunch with Will every day, with Alice glaring at them from her spot on the bench. Clara and Anthony had dinner together several nights a week, but he had never again asked her to hang out with his frat buddies. While this relieved her, it also worried her. Had she done something to embarrass him? Did he not want her around his friends anymore? Try as she might, Clara couldn't get the thought out of her head that something felt off.

By the end of the week, Clara was no closer to finding any clues. The knife had come back with no evidence on it besides Kelly Jo's blood, meaning the killer had probably worn gloves. Of course, if the killer was a cop, that made sense. They would know to do that. During one of their lunches, Clara vented to Will. "I just feel like I've hit a wall. I mean, I think every time I open a box, this one will be it. This will be the box that tells me what I need to know. And every time, it's the same thing. Nothing."

Will took a bite of his taco. "I mean, there are so many boxes in there. Did you really expect to find the answer in the first ten?"

Clara rolled her eyes, munching on carrots. She had grown tired of tacos and had started bringing her own lunch. "I honestly did. I thought it would be easy. I was very wrong." She leaned against the tree and closed her eyes.

"Don't look now, but she's doing it again."

Clara's eyes snapped open and she turned her head.

"I said don't look."

Alice sat on her bench with her two female cohorts and looked in their direction. She ate her food as slowly as possible, waiting for Will and Clara to finish. "Why does she sit and stare at us every day? It's creepy," Clara said.

Will shrugged. "To get us to do what she wants."

Clara looked over at him. "Which is?"

"React to her. She wants us to go over there and demand to know what her problem is. If we ignore her, she'll eventually stop."

"I don't know. I think she'll stop once I leave."

He turned to her, meeting her gaze. "Will you leave?"

She nodded. "I have to at some point. I start classes in the spring. I can't stay here and go to school. That's a lot of work for one person to do."

He scratched the back of his neck, his cheeks reddening. "I get that. It's just going to be weird without you here."

Clara shoved his shoulder, trying to smile. "We have plenty of time before that happens. Remember, I have a murder to solve."

"Speaking of, hear anything that might help?"

Clara shook her head, feeling defeated. "Nope. Which is weird. As soon as I walk into the room, people stop talking around me. That's definitely not normal."

Will looked back over at Alice. "Do you think she has anything to do with it?"

Clara had a sneaking suspicion that she did. "Maybe. But I don't know how to change that." She stood up and brushed off her black pencil skirt. "Thank you for another lovely lunch, Will."

He stood and gave her a mock bow. "The pleasure is all mine, milady."

Clara giggled and shook her head as she went back inside the precinct.

While Will took the elevator back to the squad room, Clara stood at the front desk, waiting for Alice. It was time they had a heart to heart.

Alice stomped in and didn't even look up as she brushed past Clara. She slammed into her chair and folded her arms across her chest. When Alice finally looked up, her eyebrows shot up into her hairline. "What do you want?" The question came out more like a growl than actual words.

"We need to talk. You seem mad at me and I'm not really sure why."

"You ruined my chances with Will."

Clara quirked a single eyebrow. "I ruined your chances? Alice, you barely spoke to him all night. Then when you did speak, you said things that normal people don't say out loud."

"Like what?"

"Alice, even if you pretended to not know how to play the game so you could read my body language cues, which is pretty freaking smart by the way, you don't actually tell anyone you're doing that. It makes other people feel stupid and it can be quite embarrassing. It embarrassed Will."

"So that's why he won't go out with me again?"

Clara sighed and leaned against the desk. "Alice, maybe you two just aren't compatible. I mean, you didn't even try to get to know him. Why didn't you say anything?"

"My daddy always said that a woman should be silent." Alice mumbled this, making Clara strain to hear.

"Well, how does your daddy expect men to get to know you if you don't say anything?"

Alice dropped her face into her hands. "He doesn't. If he had his way, I wouldn't date at all." She looked up at Clara, anger flashing in her eyes. "But Daddy doesn't control me. I'm an adult."

A chill went up Clara's spine. The way Alice said those words, the coldness of her voice … Clara could never imagine speaking of her parents like that. "Yes, you are. Maybe Will just needs time. You could try a peace offering."

"A what?" Alice didn't even try to hide her confusion.

"A peace offering. Bring something you think he'll like, something that will help him see you're sorry for making him uncomfortable. Like cookies or brownies."

"I can do brownies. Do I just bring them in?"

Clara nodded. "And leave them on his desk with a little 'I'm sorry' note." She paused, trying to come up with the right words. "Alice, what have you been telling people about me?"

Alice's head snapped up. Her earlier confusion and anger were gone. Instead, her face paled, making the redness of her cheeks stand out even more. "Excuse me?"

"People get oddly quiet around me. Someone had to have said something. Was it you?"

Alice nodded once. "I did. I was mad at you."

"What did you tell them?" Clara tried to keep her voice even, not letting her anger show.

She shrugged. "Just that you're trying to steal Will from me and that the fiancé is all a lie and doesn't actually exist. And that if you don't get Will, you'll go after one of the other guys. That the only reason you're really here is to end up married to a cop." Alice took a deep breath and bit her lip.

"Alice." Clare couldn't keep the hurt from her voice. "Why?"

"I was mad at you after Will blew me off. He didn't want to see me anymore and I blamed you. If you hadn't invited us over, things would've been different." Alice was twisting her hands now, rubbing them together.

"You really think that? Alice, you have to talk to Will to get him to ask you out again. Not only did you hardly speak to him at my place, but then, after he asked to be just friends, you sat and stared at him every day during lunch. It's creepy."

For the first time, Clara saw Alice give her a genuine smile. "I know. That was kind of the point. I was trying to get a reaction out of him." She gave Clara a once-over. "Guess I got a reaction out of you instead."

Clara blew out a hard breath. "Look, try to act normal and maybe he'll start talking to you again, OK? I can't guarantee he'll ever ask you out again, but a peace offering can't hurt, can it?"

Alice shrugged. "I'll give it a shot."

Clara nodded and headed to the elevator. She turned back with one last thought. "Quell the rumors about me. Say you were mistaken. OK?"

Alice just nodded, not even bothering to look from up her desk.

Clara stepped into the elevator, not sure there was much else she could do.

***

Clara was sifting through another box of evidence, cataloging each file and piece of evidence, when she finally blurted out, "Alice is crazy."

Morgan looked up at her, newspaper in hand. "What?"

Clara sighed and rested her hand on the box. "Alice is crazy. Like, loony crazy. I can't believe someone like her passed all the evaluations."

Morgan snapped the paper and turned back to it. "You'd be surprised who passes those things."

Clara put her hands on her hips and blew a strand of hair out of her face. "Well, I think it's ridiculous. She's insane and that doesn't seem to bother anyone."

"She's at the front desk. What harm can she do there?"

"Not transfer a call?"

"Everything goes through a switchboard. She doesn't actually answer calls until they've been transferred to her."

Clara deflated. "Something is just off about her. I don't know what it is."

"A lot of us chalk it up to her partner dying. It was a pretty traumatic experience. In a moment when she was tested as a cop, she failed. It ended in her partner's death. Afterward, no one really wanted to partner with her. She was also very depressed and gloomy at the time."

"Well, her partner had died. That's understandable."

"No, that's not why she was gloomy. She was worried about who she would be partnered with next. She tried to pick her partner instead of waiting to be assigned. She followed people around for days, then spent several days after that lamenting how much she didn't want to be their partner. It got so bad that the captain relegated her to the front desk so she'd leave everyone alone."

Clara picked up the next file and flipped it open. "Did that help?"

"It stopped her from bothering the rest of us. So I guess so."

Clara scanned the page in front of her. Halfway down, her finger stopped. Something was odd about this evidence list. "Morgan, didn't you say that the case with the knife was your case?"

He set down the paper. "Yeah, why?"

"The knife is listed again." She handed him the list. "Doesn't that sound like the same knife?"

He skimmed the description and looked back up at her. "Yeah, it does. But how is that even possible? We don't give back evidence like that."

Clara sat down and clasped her hands in front of her. "Tell me about your case. How did you find the knife?"

He rubbed his leg and set the list on his desk. "The kid I was arresting pulled it on me, stabbed me in the leg with it, and attempted to run off. It was a drug bust, just a couple kids we wanted to sweat to get info on who was supplying them. I shot him in the leg to stop him from getting away."

"So that's how you were injured?"

He nodded. "He did quite a bit of damage in there. I'll always have a limp, standing for long periods hurts, and it aches when it rains now. But that doesn't mean I'm useless."

Clara held up her hands. "I believe you." She pointed at the list. "Wanna take a look and see if there's a duplicate knife back there? Because it's not in the box."

Morgan nodded and headed back into the cage. Clara could hear him rummaging around. Boxes were dropped to the floor and they scraped against the concrete floor. After ten minutes of this, he reappeared, empty-handed. "There's no knife back there for that case number."

Clara chewed on her bottom lip, thinking. "So it's the same knife. But how?" Clara pulled out the report and scanned the top page. Morgan stood over her shoulder, reading too. "This was a murder committed before Kelly Jo died." She looked up at Morgan. "Do you remember anything about this?"

He took the report and flipped through it. "Ralph caught this one. Nothing to it, really. Some old coot living in a trailer out in the sticks dies and sits there stinking up the place for a couple days. Neighbor goes to check on him, finds him, and calls it in. Knife stuck in his leg, severed the femoral artery. Neighbor claims he liked to carry it around, show it off to people or threaten them with it, depending on who they were."

"So that knife gets brought in here, logged as evidence, and locked up. How does it end up back on the street?"

Morgan rubbed a hand over his face. "Someone took it." He started pacing, his hands flying around his head. "Somehow, someone broke in here and got it out. Before Kelly Jo died, security

143

wasn't as tight as it is now. I'm sure the captain told you that. We had to sign a log to check things out, and we had the security cameras, but there were blind spots. The guy who ran this before me, he was getting up in years, started getting forgetful. He had been with us for as long as I could remember. Letting him go was the hardest thing the captain ever had to do."

"Do you think someone pretended to log it and just took it? Or snuck it past him?"

Morgan nodded. "It's a big possibility. And he wouldn't remember if they did or not."

Clara looked down at the file. "Why this knife? What's so special about it?" Her head snapped up. "Do you think maybe Kelly Jo was killed because she caught them taking the knife? Maybe it had nothing to do with the fact that she was cataloging stuff."

Morgan followed her train of thought. "She stayed up here during lunches while I was outside. They could've easily come in, claimed to be looking for something for a case, and gone back to the cage that Kelly Jo would've opened for them. She could have gone to check on them later only to find them attempting to take the knife. The fact that it happened in a blind spot was just coincidence."

"But wouldn't you guys have seen them on the tapes anyway? Seen them enter and leave?"

He shook his head. "No one but the captain and I know this, so don't you go repeating it, but there was a glitch that day. Not only was Kelly Jo killed in the blind spot, but the cameras were down for several hours before and after her murder. They came back on after lunch was over, but I didn't find Kelly Jo until I went looking for her. She was lying in the blind spot, so she didn't show up on the camera. I thought she had gone to grab lunch offsite, not thinking she was back there, dying." His hands shook as he said this and his eyes misted.

Clara placed one hand on his. "The knife is the key. If we figure out why it's so important, we may figure out who did this." She took the report back from him. Then she pulled out a yellow notepad and began scribbling information from the report. "I'm going to do some more research this weekend. See what I can find out about this guy. There's a reason someone took this knife. I want to know why."

Clara spent the rest of the afternoon cataloging the rest of the box. Nothing else was missing, but Clara had a feeling the knife wouldn't be the last piece of evidence she'd find in the wrong place. Something fishy was going on and she was going to get to the bottom of it.

10.

SURPRISE VISIT

Clara got to her apartment that evening to find that Anthony had stopped by and left a bouquet of roses on her table. A note attached to them read, "I love you more than anything else. Dinner tomorrow night?" Clara grinned. He must've gotten the night off and he wanted to spend the evening with her instead of his frat buddies.

She popped a frozen meal into her microwave. Tonight, she would research and figure out who that guy was. Find out as much information about him as she could. That way, she could focus on Anthony tomorrow and not worry about the case. As she munched on her dinner, she realized that sometimes she could be a little obsessive when it came to cases like this and that Anthony wasn't quite used to it. She hadn't had to solve any murders back home since his brother had been locked up.

Clara booted up her laptop and pulled the yellow notepad from her purse. At the top of the page, she had scribbled the man's name: Ernest Williams. She decided to start there, using his date of birth to see what she could dig up on him. The rest of her food cooled as she sat clicking through web pages and scribbling more notes on her pad. Ernest Williams may have been crazy, but he had certainly led an interesting life.

Ernest had been born not too far away. He grew up in the area, then enlisted in the Army in 1969. He wasn't drafted—he actually enlisted. Did two tours in Vietnam, came home a pretty decorated soldier, then settled back into life here. Except settling never really happened. His obituary mentioned some run-ins with the law. There also seemed to be two ex-wives, one of whom had a baby with Ernest, but left him shortly after the baby was born. Try as she could, Clara couldn't find any information about the child. Clara made a note on her pad to ask Morgan to look up Ernest's police record on Monday. That might shed some light on what had gone on in his life. Clara suspected heavy drinking was probably involved.

Sitting back in her chair, she looked at her clock. It was well past midnight. Clara decided that she had found all she was going to find on Ernest that night. She closed the laptop and headed to her room only to stop at the sound of a knock on her door. Checking her clock again, Clara sighed. Someone showing up this late couldn't be good. She checked her peephole, then almost fell over in shock. Throwing open the door, she yanked three bodies inside, crushing them in a hug. "What are you guys doing here?"

Tracy laughed and pushed away first. "Anthony called, said you seemed lonely. We decided to visit for the weekend."

Hannah blew her bangs out of her eyes. "Yeah, he said there was a party tomorrow night and that we could talk you into being a sociable person."

Stacy kissed Clara's cheek. "And we missed you."

Clara hugged her friends again, tears coming to her eyes. While she was happy to see them, she felt slightly hurt that Anthony had called them in to get her to go to another frat party. So she and Anthony would be spending tomorrow night together, but not in the way Clara thought they would. Pushing aside those thoughts, she pulled back and grinned at them. "A weekend visit, huh? What about your families?" She looked at Stacy. "And Rodney?"

Hannah rolled her grey eyes. "Pssh. Our families see us pretty regularly. Not all of us went that far from home."

Stacy giggled, pulling on a piece of auburn hair. "Rodney will be fine. He said you needed me more and that he was willing to share, but you had to give me back at the end of the weekend."

Clara laughed, love for her older brother filling her heart. "Well, then, let's get you girls settled in."

As they unpacked their bags and set up camp in Clara's small living room, she filled them in on the developments at the precinct so far.

"So, you found the murder weapon?" Hanna sounded impressed.

Into the living room, Clara brought a tray with sweet tea and glasses on it. "I did. At the bottom of one of the boxes. It still had her blood on it, too."

"How do you think it ended up there?" Stacy took a glass and poured tea into it.

"Well, that was the box Kelly Jo had been working on when she died. My assumption is that the killer freaked out, stashed it in the box, dumped all the files on top, and prayed no one would find it."

Hannah leaned back and stretched out her long legs. "And apparently they never bothered to look in there? What kind of crackpot police force is this?"

Clara patted Hannah's knee. "Not everyone is as good as our dads are. I also don't think they considered the box part of evidence since she wasn't murdered anywhere near it."

Tracy snorted, her small nose wrinkling. "Well, now they know better."

A brief silence fell over them. Then Hannah burst out, "So, how did things go with your matchmaking?"

Clara flinched. "Ugh, Alice. Guys, she's nuts. I'm pretty sure she lied through her psych eval."

Hannah gave a "come on" gesture. "Explain."

Clara told them about the double date and Alice's response to winning the game. Then she told them about the creepy staring and the conversation they'd had. "It's like she doesn't really understand social cues. Almost like she copies the people around her until it doesn't suit her anymore."

"And Will?"

Clara smiled. "He's sweet. Morgan asked him to keep an eye on me when I first got there, which I didn't take very well. It felt like a betrayal, but Morgan explained that Will probably would've done it anyway if he hadn't asked. Morgan just pushed him a little earlier than is normal for Will."

The three girls leaned back, their full attention on Clara. "You like Will." Stacy said it as a statement, not a question.

Clara fidgeted with her ring. "I mean, he's a nice guy. And funny. We're friends."

"Does Anthony know you like him?" Hannah raised one perfect eyebrow.

Clara shrugged. "He's met him. He knows we're friends and that we eat lunch together. It doesn't seem to bother him."

Stacy grimaced. "He's still spending all his time with the frat, isn't he?"

Clara nodded. "Where do you think that party is tomorrow night?"

All three girls groaned. "We wouldn't have said yes if we had known that." Stacy threw a pillow at the empty couch.

Clara held up her hands. "It's OK. It's not your fault and it's really not his, either. I've been very unwilling to get involved in that part of his life and that's unfair of me. I just need to make more of an effort." She looked at the clock. "But if we want to be functioning human beings tomorrow, we really should get some sleep." Clara went to her room and reemerged with an armful of blankets and pillows. Hannah moved the coffee table out of the way so that Clara could spread everything out on the floor in front of the TV. They settled down together on the floor, blankets and pillows surrounding them, the TV playing in the background. Clara smiled as she fell asleep, happy to have her friends with her.

11.

FRAT PARTY TAKE TWO

The next day was spent at a Waffle House getting breakfast, then shopping for new outfits for the party that night. Clara realized she hadn't been shopping for non-apartment-related stuff since she'd moved in. She smiled as Tracy twirled in front of the full-length mirror in a short green dress. "The boys will eat you up in that." Clara tried to lighten the words with a grin.

Tracy winked at her. "That's the point." She slipped back into the changing room. "I'll take this one."

Clara narrowed her eyes at the door behind which Tracy had disappeared. "What about the frat boy you mentioned?"

Tracy poked her head back out of the door and wrinkled her nose at Clara. "That fizzled out."

Clara looked down at the bags in her hands. She had managed to find a cute pleated blue skirt and a red tank top with a dipped neckline that she really liked. Add white sandals and the girls had declared her ready for a Fourth of July party. Deciding that it might be a little much, she had also purchased a white top of the same type, to wear on non-holiday weekends.

On their way out of the mall, the girls stopped to get coffee. As they did, they discussed their outfits. "I'll be in all red." Hannah grinned as she took her coffee from the barista.

Stacy flipped her auburn hair over her shoulder. "Jeans and a blue tank top. I'm not trying to attract attention."

"Yeah, don't want to worry Rodney too much." Tracy giggled, hoisting up her bag. "I've got the green dress."

"And I'm in the skirt and top."
Clara took her coffee and inhaled its
heady aroma. They walked out to the car,
the afternoon sun warming their backs as
they did.

"So, Clara, are any of these guys
attractive?" Tracy tried to act like she
wasn't curious.

Clara shrugged. "They aren't bad,
if you like that sort of thing."

Hannah swung around and
stopped in front of Clara. "What sort of
thing?"

"I mean, they're all buff and tall, I
guess. Very frat-boy-ish."

Hannah groaned. "Clara, your
fiancé is very frat-boy-ish, if you hadn't
noticed."

Clara dropped her eyes. Her
cheeks reddened. "I know."

They got into the car in silence, all
lost in thought. Stacy was the first to
break it. "If you don't like the frat, why
don't you say something?"

"I have. Every time I do, he tells me that I'm too judgmental, that I don't give them a chance." Clara looked into her rearview. "He's not wrong. I've been against it from the get-go. I've been to only one party. Maybe I need to just give it a chance."

"Or maybe your instincts are telling you something." Hannah gave her a knowing look—a look that children of police officers gave each other. They learned from an early age that if your gut was telling you something, it was usually right.

Clara shook her head. "I just need to try harder. I will try harder." She kept her eyes on the road, not seeing the other girls share a look riddled with worry.

Back at the apartment, they showered and changed into their outfits. "Anthony said the party doesn't start until after 8 p.m." Stacy rapped her fingers on the counter. "We have an hour. What do we do with it?"

"Food?" Hannah opened the freezer. "I'm starving."

"You're always starving." Tracy pushed her out of the way, her green dress sparkling in the kitchen light.

Clara reached around them and pulled out a box of frozen mozzarella sticks. "How about these? We make the whole box and that should tide us over. I have ranch." After a chorus of agreements, Clara nuked the sticks in the microwave. The girls devoured them in less than five minutes.

Clara finally agreed that they could head to the party. "We may be a little early, but I don't think that will matter."

Finding a place to park seemed to be the hardest part. Clara had to park three blocks from the frat house, and she grumbled about having to walk in heels. The girls pulled her along, making jokes the whole way. When they reached the house, the music was going full blast, the ground vibrating with the beat. They opened the front door to find people milling around, red Solo cups in hand.

Clara pushed past them, her head whipping around. "I didn't realize there would be so many people here already." Again, the three girls shared a worried look behind her back.

In the living room, the guys all stood around the fireplace, their heads close together as they talked. Jay was the first to notice the girls. His easy smile popped onto his face. "Clara! So good to see you." He went in for a hug, throwing Clara off.

"Um, Jay, yeah, good to see you too. Is Anthony here?"

Charlie leaned in, his dark eyes flashing. "He's out back, I think. We got a DJ to come in, so he's helping set up back there."

Darren's green eyes snapped to Hannah. Her short red skirt was drawing his attention. "I can take you back there."

Clara nodded. Her hands gripped her small purse for dear life. This didn't feel right. Anthony should've met her at the door. Clara's stomach rolled with nerves.

On the back porch, a DJ stood behind his booth, pulling out CDs and organizing his equipment. Darren leaned in to ask a question. The DJ pointed toward the pool, so Darren headed that way, the girls following. Groups of people were gathered around the outdoor pool, some dancing in groups, others sitting in lawn chairs, drinking from cups. Clara spotted Anthony first, chatting with a short blonde. He turned as they approached and he smiled. "Hey, you guys made it!"

Darren stepped back, giving them room. The girls all gave him a hug, Clara going last. Her eyes followed the girl, watching as she went up to the DJ booth. Darren watched Clara, noticing her gaze. Anthony took her chin in his hand and turned her face back to him. "Hey, Earth to Clara?"

"Who is she?" Clara bit her lip, knowing the minute she said the words that they were the wrong ones to say. Anthony could have friends who weren't her. It just hurt that he wouldn't tell her about them.

"That's Hailey. She's in one of the sororities and she helps us throw parties sometimes. I think you'd like her." He looked up to find Hannah, Stacy, and Tracy all shaking their heads, giving him "abort" signals. He bit his cheek. "But right now I want to spend time with you. Tell me what you've been up to. Any breaks in the case?" At his question, Clara's face lit up like a thousand lights at Christmas time. She started telling him about the knife and how it had been part of three cases, including Kelly Jo's murder. Her hands flew as she talked. The girls relaxed, happy to see Clara distracted.

Darren leaned in closer to Hannah, his mouth against her ear. "When she talks about that stuff, she really looks like a different person. Makes her look even prettier than she already is."

Hannah grinned. "That's our girl. Solving crime is her jam."

"What about you? What's your jam?"

Hannah looked into his green eyes, almost getting lost in them. She blinked several times to clear her head. "I prefer science. I think solving crimes is important, but most of the time it comes down to science to put the criminal behind bars."

Darren crossed his arms, his muscles bulging in his polo shirt. "Oh, really? Science, huh?"

She nodded, her eyes still on Clara. "Microbiology is fascinating. I'm going to school to be a forensic scientist."

Clara pulled back from Anthony and looked at the girls. "Are you guys thirsty? Do you want something to drink?"

At their nods, Clara kissed Anthony on the cheek, then led them back inside to the kitchen for punch. Hannah locked eyes with Hailey as they walked past, holding her gaze until they were inside. With her blonde hair and clear blue eyes, Hailey was definitely a looker. And she didn't back down when Hannah made eye contact.

Clara handed each girl a cup, then took one for herself. "So, what do you think?"

Stacy looked around the kitchen. "This is a huge house. They all live here together?"

Clara nodded. "A house full of men."

Tracy wrinkled her nose. "It probably gets smelly in here." The other girls laughed, imagining how bad the smell could be. Tracy sniffed. "Not too bad right now. They must've cleaned."

Clara locked eyes with Hannah. "Well?"

Hannah sighed. "I'm not sure. They seem nice enough. But that Hailey chick? She wants something. She doesn't seem scared of anything. Actually, she seems pretty confident about being in this house."

"That would be because she dated some of us for a bit."

The girls turned to find Jay standing in the doorway, empty cup in hand.

"I just came in for a refill."

Clare turned bright red, her face burning. "I'm so sorry. We didn't mean anything by it."

He shrugged, his short hair glistening in the kitchen light. "Nah, I get it. You don't know us, you don't know anyone here, and Anthony has been spending a lot of time with us. It's normal to be suspicious." He took a sip of punch. "How about I fill you in on some of the details?" At the girl's nods, he continued. "Hailey has dated all of us, actually, except Anthony. She started off with Jaxon, during the first half of freshman year. Didn't last very long. They were pretty volatile together. Then she moved on to Darren and broke his heart. That was a long summer, helping him get over her. Show up at school in the fall to find her with Charlie, hanging on his arm, walking to class with him. Charlie had one thing on his mind and when he got it, he dumped her."

Tracy leaned in and looked into his eyes, which at the moment looked more blue than green. "And you?"

He shrugged. "I was the last one. We went on a couple dates but I knew pretty early on I wasn't interested. I really strung her along because I was still mad at her for breaking Darren's heart like she did. She wasn't happy when I told her I was no longer interested."

"And Anthony?" Hannah didn't mince words. She wanted to get to the bottom of this.

Jay looked toward the backyard. "Anthony is unavailable and she knows that. He makes it no secret that he's going to marry the love of his life. But that doesn't stop her from attempting to go at him every chance she gets." He leaned in, like what he had to say next was a secret. "I think she thought he was lying until tonight, since she had never seen you before."

Clara's shoulders slumped. "That's my fault. I haven't been around here enough to really prove I exist." She looked up at the ceiling. "I just don't feel like I belong here."

Jay held up his hands in mock surrender. "Do any of us?" Giving them a nod, he left the room.

The girls stared at each other for a minute. "His honesty is refreshing." Clara could hear the admiration in Hannah's voice.

"He's going to join the military, Hannah."

She shrugged. "And I've got a lot of college to get through. Maybe we can be pen pals."

The other girls laughed but Clara kept silent and looked toward the back. "I've really been a crappy fiancée, haven't I?"

The girls shook their heads. "No. You just needed time to adjust. This is a new experience. Now that you know you need to be here, you will." Clara wished she could share Stacy's confidence.

"I just don't know that I can. Like, I'm not a partier. Spending my weekends here isn't my idea of fun. I didn't think it was Anthony's, either." She watched through the back door as Hailey walked up to Anthony, her bathing suit cover-up not really doing its job. Hailey pressed her body against his as Anthony tried to step away from her. "He doesn't seem to mind it like I thought he would."

"He's never been in this situation before. Can you blame him for liking all the attention he's getting?" Tracy followed Clara's gaze, grimacing as Hailey made another pass at Anthony.

Clara set down her drink. "I think I need to set some boundaries out there." She marched out, leaving the girls to watch in shock as she pushed Hailey aside to pull Anthony into a long kiss, wrapping her body around his. Anthony melted into her while Hailey stood, arms crossed, a dirty look on her face. Darren had the presence of mind to grab Hailey by the shoulders and pull her away before Anthony or Clara looked up and caught her staring.

When they separated, the goofiest grin the girls had ever seen was covering Anthony's face. Clara's hand trailed along his arm as she stepped away and headed back to the kitchen. She looked at their surprised faces and smiled herself. "Just, um, staking my claim."

"More like marking your territory. Nice move." Hannah sounded impressed.

"She'll think twice, that's for sure." Tracy sounded more confident than Clara felt.

"I just don't get why she's making her way through all the guys. What self-respecting girl does that?"

Stacy shook her head. "None. But I don't think she's a self-respecting girl." They fell into an easy silence, broken only by Anthony, who came charging into the kitchen, declaring it was time to dance.

Clara stepped out onto the back porch to find that a covering had been placed over the pool. Through the opaque cover, she could see the water as it rippled. Different-colored lights flashed underwater. Clara looked at Anthony.

"You can dance on the cover. Trust me." He held out a hand, waiting for her. She took it and allowed him to pull her onto the cover. Looking back at the girls, she smiled. They seemed to be enjoying themselves.

Within minutes, each of the girls had joined her. Jay had grabbed Hannah and was spinning her around the edge of the cover. Charlie held Tracy close, whispering something in her ear. Darren and Stacy danced off to the side, neither getting very close to the other. Anthony smiled. "Darren has a girlfriend. She's studying abroad this semester, so he's been kind of grumpy."

Clara turned and wrapped her arms around his neck. She rested her head on his chest, right against his

171

collarbone. His hands came around her, holding her tightly against him. She sighed, enjoying the feeling. This was where she most liked to be, pressed against him, in a spot she felt had been created just for her.

"I love you." He whispered it into her hair, for only her to hear.

"I love you too," she whispered against his chest. At that moment, she felt like all was right with the world. Whatever issues she'd had with him being in the frat seemed to disappear.

12.

COINCIDENCES

The following afternoon, Clara dropped the girls off at the airport. All three promised to text when their planes touched down, and each hugged her close before walking inside. Clara brushed tears from her eyes as she pulled away from the curb, trying to keep it together. They wouldn't be apart forever. This was only temporary and it would pass.

Her apartment felt empty without her friends in it. Anthony was working, so Clara cleaned up the pillows and blankets, then stacked the glasses and plates in the dishwasher. Having them here had been something she hadn't realized she needed until they'd showed up. Now she was unsure what to do with her time.

The girls had spent all morning talking about the party, their voices filling

173

Clara's apartment. Hannah had adored Jay, going on and on about his eyes. Tracy had found Charlie to be very fetching and had spent most of the morning talking about the texts they were sharing back and forth. Only Stacy didn't seem to be as enthusiastic. While the other two giggled together, she had pulled Clara aside. "They're nice guys and all, but I'm getting a feeling that I don't like. The fact that they all dated that Hailey chick, even after what she pulled with the first one, just struck me as weird. Is it, like, an initiation thing that they have to date her? And if that's the case, where does that leave Anthony, since he's engaged to you?"

Clara had agreed, unsure where to go from there. The guys had been nothing but nice to her and her friends, yet there she was, still doubting and judging them. Maybe Hailey just had a way with them that Clara didn't understand. She wanted nothing more than for Stacy to be wrong. Even Hannah had been convinced that they were OK but Clara suspected that had more to do with Jay's smile and eyes than anything else.

She pulled out her laptop and decided to do some more research. If nothing else, it would certainly help distract her. Clara decided to start looking for Ernest's long-lost child. First, she would have to figure out the wife's maiden name. Tapping a finger against her lips, she closed her eyes, trying to think about how to do this. Her best bet would probably be marriage announcements in the paper. She searched the web, looking to see if the town's newspaper had been transferred to digital. Lo and behold, there happened to be an archive of the newspaper. She typed in Ernest's name, hoping to get a hit.

Clara's mouth hung open as the articles popped up on her screen. The first article depicted Ernest receiving an award after having come back from Vietnam. Another article showed him and his first wife, a Martha Nalle, walking out of a church together. Then, several years later, another picture, similar to the last, of Ernest walking out of church with another woman. This woman, Emma Wheeler, looked quite a bit younger than Ernest did. Clara suspected the baby may have been the reason for such a marriage. In this wedding photo, Ernest wasn't the dashing war hero anymore. Time and drinking had aged him.

Clara decided to see if she could find any more information about Emma Wheeler. Much to her surprise, Emma had a Facebook profile. Clara almost fell out of her chair. The woman had more friends than Clara knew in real life. As Clara clicked through Emma's profile, she found pictures with grandchildren, a life filled with love and happiness. Not one mention of Ernest anywhere. Chewing on her bottom lip, Clara decided to take a chance. How could a conversation hurt? She sent Emma a message, asking if she minded answering a few questions. Clara didn't expect to get an immediate response, but within five minutes of sending the message, Emma had sent one back. She wrote that she would love to chat, but that she preferred the phone to Messenger. She gave Clara her number.

Clara pulled out her cell phone and dialed Emma's number. She prayed that Emma would be able to answer her questions. The phone rang three times. Then a wispy voice answered. "Hello?"

"Ms. Wheeler? It's Clara. I sent you a message earlier?"

"Yes, my dear, that's me. What can I do for you?"

Clara took a deep breath. "I'm calling to ask you about your first husband, Ernest Williams. I was wondering if you would mind talking about him."

"Oh my. I haven't thought about Ernest in years. I married him when I was barely sixteen."

Clara made a note on her pad. "Why was that?"

Emma paused, then said quietly, "I was in the family way. It's what we did back then, dear."

Clara thought a moment, then plunged ahead. "And the child?"

"I had a bouncing baby boy. Most beautiful baby you ever saw." Another pause, this one longer. Clara held her breath, waiting for Emma to continue. "They took him from me, you know." Her voice cracked, the last word barely above a whisper.

"Who took him from you?" Clara scribbled more on her pad. She felt like she was finally getting somewhere.

"The state. I left Ernest shortly after the baby was born. He drank heavily and got very abusive. But if you're asking about Ernest, you probably already know that. My family wouldn't take me back. They told me that I should stay with my husband. I knew that if I did that, I and my son might die, so I had to come up with other options. Ernest didn't care what I did. He even signed over his parental rights. So, I gave the baby up for adoption, hoping to give him a better chance than I ever had."

"Oh, Emma. I'm sure he did. Do you remember who adopted him?"

A rustling sound crackled over the line. "It's been so long. They were an older couple, hadn't been able to have children of their own. Good Christian people. Let me think a minute." More rustling, then silence. "Carver. The last name was Carver. They promised to take really good care of him."

Clara scribbled Carver on her pad and circled it several times. "I'm sure they did, Ms. Wheeler. Is there anything else you can tell me about Ernest?"

"Besides the fact that he liked to drink, he really liked to hunt. Had a knife that he used to cut up the animals he killed, favorite knife of his. Couldn't part that thing from him for nothing. I swore he would cut me up with it one day."

"Was it serrated? Black handle?"

"Well, my goodness, yes it was. How did you know?"

"I hate to be the bearer of bad news, Ms. Wheeler, but Ernest died several years ago. He stabbed himself by accident with that knife and bled out."

Ms. Wheeler's gasp on the other end of the line took Clara by surprise. "Poor Ernest."

"Excuse me?"

Ms. Wheeler must've heard the confusion in Clara's voice because she began to explain. "Clara, darling, Ernest had his faults, don't get me wrong. The man had demons that no one knew how to get rid of. But I still loved him. I planned a life with him. He made an effort for a time, but those demons won in the end. Just because I haven't seen him in years doesn't mean I don't still care for him."

Clara nodded, realizing that the other woman couldn't see her. "Yes, ma'am, I understand. Thank you for your time." Ms. Wheeler wished her a good day and Clara hung up.

She looked at her notepad. Carver was an unusual name, and it sounded so familiar. Clara couldn't place where she had heard it recently. Looking at the clock, she realized that she should probably eat something before heading to bed. She did have to be at work bright and early in the morning.

Too drained to cook anything, she instead ate a ham sandwich, which she washed down with water. Then she headed to bed. That last name kept tugging at her brain. She hoped that it would come to her in her sleep. Clara climbed into bed and pulled the covers up to her chin. She closed her eyes and let her mind drift. Snapshots from the weekend flooded her senses. Words and sounds came to the forefront. As she slipped deeper into sleep, Clara heard a voice repeating "Carver" over and over again. She just couldn't put her finger on where she had heard it before.

***

While waiting to get on the elevator the next morning, Clara felt

Alice's eyes bore into her back. Clara was still trying to work out the mystery of where she had heard the name Carver before. Just as the elevator popped open, she heard a voice call her name. Something in her mind snapped and she spun around to see Will walking toward her, donuts in one hand, coffee in the other. She grabbed his arm and yanked him into the elevator. "We need to talk."

He looked at her, puzzled. "About?" He shifted his hold on the donuts and offered her the coffee. She took the holder and looked up at him.

"Carver."

He tilted his head. "Harry?"

"Yes, that Carver." The elevator opened and Clara grabbed Will's arm again. She pulled him down the hall to Evidence. There, she threw open the door, having already handed the coffee back to him. Clara tossed her purse on the desk and waited until Will had set down the coffee and donuts before continuing. Morgan leaned back in his chair, preparing for a long conversation.

"I talked to Ernest Williams' second ex-wife yesterday. Learned some pretty interesting things."

"Like?" Morgan didn't seem impressed.

"She said he was a drunk, that he had demons he couldn't escape. She said they tried to make it work but he couldn't get past the war. They had a child together but when she left Ernest, she had no other options. She had to give that child up for adoption, to a family named Carver." Clara looked at Will.

"Harry? When was this child born?" Will sounded skeptical.

Clara ignored the question. "Will, the knife used to kill Kelly Jo? It was originally this Ernest guy's knife. He stabbed himself with it on accident and died. Then, someone took it from Evidence and gave it to the kid who stabbed Morgan. It was the same knife in both cases."

"But what does that have to do with Harry?"

"What if Harry figured out Ernest was his dad and came in here to look through his things? Took the knife as a keepsake?"

Morgan held up a hand. "Except that Harry is too young to be Ernest's son." Before Clara could protest, he continued. "That child was born in the 70s. Harry is a 90s baby."

"So, grandson? Maybe he's Ernest's grandson."

"While that's a possibility, why would he take the knife? To have some connection to a person he never even knew?" Now Will really didn't sound convinced.

Clara sighed. "We could ask him."

Morgan shook his head. "No way. We're going to follow this trail, but we start with the father. Confirm he was the baby given up for adoption. Then we go from there. No sense throwing Harry for a loop if we don't have to."

Clara agreed and sat down at her desk, all her fire gone. What had started as a huge discovery now felt very hollow.

Will picked up the donuts, left a coffee for her, and exited the room without another word. Clara watched him leave, sadness seeping into her bones.

"He's mad at me, isn't he?"

Morgan followed her gaze, his softening. "Disappointed is more like it. At the very least, you accused one of his friends of tampering with evidence. At the most, you accused him of murder. It's going to take him a while to come to terms with that."

She looked at Morgan. "And you? What do you think?"

He crossed his arms and looked at the ceiling. "I think that anyone is capable of anything. Harry may have taken the knife out of pure curiosity about the man it had belonged to. And then lost it. While that's wrong, it's not devious or evil."

185

"But do you think that he came back here that day to get it? Knowing it had been brought in as evidence?"

Morgan shook his head. "Harry was eating lunch with me and Ralph that day. Like he does every day. Even if he took the knife the first time, I don't think he tried to take it the second time."

Clara nodded and booted up the computer. "So we're back to square one."

Morgan smiled. "Maybe not square one. We have a lead. That's a start. Let's just make sure it's a good one."

Clara nodded and waited as he got her another box to catalog. She hoped they would get to the bottom of this soon. It felt like they were running out of time.

13.

DINNER FOR TWO

Will didn't come out for lunch that afternoon and Clara didn't see him for the rest of the week. She figured he was still upset and she let him have his space. Clara called Emma again, asking if she could dig up any of the paperwork from the adoption. She agreed and invited Clara over for dinner. Feeling like she had no choice, Clara showed up at six on the dot, macaroni salad in hand.

The address she'd been given put her in a quaint little neighborhood near an elementary school. The houses were all lined up next to each other, cookie-cutter in appearance. Emma's house even had a white picket fence, reminding Clara of a 1950s TV show. Emma's windows held garden boxes with flowers overflowing from them. A small front porch held a swing, while white lace curtains surrounded the front window.

Standing on that porch, Clara felt like she was stepping into another world.

The woman who opened the door gave Clara a huge smile. Wrinkles lined the woman's face and surrounded her grey eyes, like she had smiled a lot in her lifetime. Wispy blonde hair had been piled on top of her head. The woman's back was straight and her gait confident.

Clara sat at the kitchen table, watching as Emma opened the macaroni salad and set it out with the other food. She had gone all out, making pork chops and Brussels sprouts. As Clara sipped sweet tea, she took in the small kitchen. There was an older black stove in the corner, a short fridge by the door, and a sink on the opposite wall under a window. Yellow curtains draped the window, matching the yellow tabletop and chairs. Even the linoleum was yellow. "You really like yellow."

Emma smiled again. "It lights up the room. Gives it a cheery feeling even on a dreary day." She scooped some macaroni salad on her plate. "Speaking of days, how was yours?"

Clara took a bite of pork chop, the meat melting in her mouth. "It was OK. One of my friends isn't talking to me and I'm not really sure how to get through to him."

"Well, what did you do to make him mad?"

Clara coughed. "What? What did I do?"

Emma shrugged her thin shoulders. The yellow fabric of her cardigan shifted with the movement. "Well, you must've done something. Why else wouldn't he be talking to you?"

Clara sighed. "You're right. I accused his friend of something and he hasn't spoken to me since. Should I apologize?" Clara found Emma surprisingly easy to confide in.

Emma smiled. "Probably. Make him see you didn't mean any harm by what you said."

Clara fidgeted with her fork. "But wouldn't he know that? I mean, I'm following the leads as they come. Is it my fault where they lead me?"

Emma reached out and took Clara's hand. "No, but it is your fault how you handle the situation. You have to realize that you aren't the only person in the world and that others can be hurt when you make rash statements."

Clara squeezed her hand. "You're one wise lady, ma'am."

A blush crept up Emma's cheeks. "I have a lot of experience rubbing people the wrong way. You remind me a little of myself when I was your age."

As Clara helped Emma clear the table and wash the dishes, she asked about the adoption papers.

"I did manage to find them." Emma seemed hesitant to continue.

Clara turned to her, dish and towel in hand. "What's wrong?"

Emma's hands were deep in the sink full of sudsy water. "I just don't want you to think badly of me, my dear. I've really enjoyed this evening and I hope that what you read doesn't change that."

Clara set down the dish and towel. She wrapped her arms around the older woman. "Now, Ms. Emma, nothing I read will change what I think of you. You don't even know what I think of you." At the slight shake of the woman's head, Clara continued. "I think you're one of the strongest people I've ever met. You were in a terrible situation as a young woman and you had to make a really hard call. You had to do what was best for you and for your child. No one can blame you for that."

Emma let Clara hold her for another minute. Then she pulled away and withdrew her hands from the water. "Then follow me." She led Clara into the living room, where a box sat on her small yellow coffee table, which sat in front of a garish yellow couch. Even the bookshelves next to the TV had been painted yellow. The white carpet and white walls made the yellow stand out even more brightly.

Clara opened the box to find a baby book on top. "I recorded everything. He was my whole world that first year."

Underneath the book, Clara found faded yellow pictures of a smiling baby with blonde hair and clear blue eyes. In a manila folder under that were the adoption papers. All they contained was Emma's information, the baby's original birth certificate, and the paperwork Emma had signed when she gave the baby to the new family. Clara looked up at Emma. "He was a year old?"

She nodded. "Almost two. It took me that long to get out of that trailer." She wiped the tears from her cheeks.

"Did you know anything about them?"

Emma sank onto the couch and looked up at Clara. "Back then, we had closed adoptions. They were going out of style but at the time I didn't see any other way to protect him, to keep him from Ernest. I went through an agency and let them pick the family. Technically, in a closed adoption, the birth mother isn't supposed to know anything about the family. For privacy." She smiled. "But the lady I worked with, she knew my situation and wanted to reassure me. She let their last name slip during one of our meetings. That's how I knew he became a Carver."

"Was that significant to you at the time? That last name?"

Emma shrugged. "They were more well-off than I was, for one. Not super-rich, but they had enough. The name drop reassured me of that. Once they adopted him, I moved on, tried to get my own life straight." She looked up at her bookshelves, which were covered with pictures of her children and grandchildren. "Guess I did a pretty good job of that."

Clara sank down next to her. "You remarried?"

Emma nodded. "Sweetest man you'd ever meet. Loved to read to me. Didn't matter what it was, he would read everything to me out loud. Loved to dance. Took me dancing up until the day he died, God rest his soul."

Clara patted her hand. "I'm so glad you were able to find happiness, Emma."

"Do you think my boy ever tried to look for me? Or Ernest?"

Clara shook her head. "I don't know. Maybe. I'm trying to figure that out. If I do find anything, I'll certainly let you know."

Emma nodded her thanks and stood. She looked at the clock on the bookshelf and her eyes widened. "Oh, my dear! I've kept you longer than I should have. I'm so sorry."

Clara jumped to her feet and pulled Emma in for another hug. "It's OK. I enjoyed tonight." As Clara headed for the door, she got an idea. "Ms. Emma, I'm not really from around here and I don't have a lot of family or friends in the area. Would you mind having dinner with me every once in a while? Only when you aren't busy?"

The smile that leaped to the older woman's face lifted Clara's soul. She could see the beautiful young woman whom Emma had once been, shining through the years. "That would be lovely. Are you sure you want to spend time with a boring old woman?"

Clara smiled at her. "Oh, Ms. Emma, I bet you're anything but boring. I look forward to seeing you again." Clara headed home, a spring in her step, with more information that she needed to process. And an apology she had to make.

14.

APOLOGIES AND MORE

The next morning, Clara waited for Will outside the precinct by the parking lot. She watched as he climbed out of his blue Camry, his tall frame making the vehicle look more like a clown car than anything else. She bit her lip and hoped she'd say the right thing to get him to accept her apology. Lunch had been awfully lonely lately.

Clara watched as he approached. His steps slowed when he noticed her leaning against the building. She had worn a long, dark blue maxi skirt with a white turtleneck and a blue scarf to match. He stopped a few feet from her, his hands hanging limply at his sides.

She looked up into his eyes, seeing the bags and the disheveled hair. "Will, I never meant to upset you. Or accuse someone you're close to. I'm just following the evidence. Isn't that what we're supposed to do? Right now, I don't have much to go on. I'm just trying to get to the bottom of it and get the right person. I would never openly accuse someone unless I was absolutely sure they were guilty."

Will's shoulders seemed to loosen slightly. "I know."

She pushed off the wall and took a step closer. "I was just so excited. I got it into my head that if I told you, then you would be as excited as I was. Then maybe we could figure it out together. I wasn't thinking about how my words would affect you."

"I know." He attempted a smile but it didn't quite reach his eyes.

"Will, what's wrong?" She reached out to touch him but stopped before she actually did. Her hand hung in the air between them.

"I asked him. Harry. I asked him if his dad had been adopted. He said yes."

197

RENEE MARSKI

Will ran a hand down his face. For the first time, Clara noticed the reddish stubble on his chin. "He said yes, Clara."

"Will, that doesn't mean anything. It doesn't mean he knows who his dad's birth parents were."

"But he does." Will's voice sounded so strained, Clara could barely make out his words. "He knows exactly who they are. He even remembers Ernest dying."

Clara took a step back and pulled her hand against her chest. "He what?"

Again with the face rub. "It was the first case he and Ralph worked together. Said he remembered the knife because of how unique it was. Didn't realize that Ernest was his grandfather."

"Will, you weren't supposed to ask him. Morgan said we were going to talk to his dad first."

"Can't. His dad died a couple years back from a heart attack. Harry is the only one left."

"But why would you ask him?"

Will threw his hands in the air. "I had to know, OK? I had to make sure he wasn't the one who did it. I wanted to see what he knew about his dad and if he knew he had been adopted. Harry knows, Clara. But I don't think he did it. I just can't figure out who would want that knife so badly." Will dropped his arms and looked down at her. "I'm not sleeping so good over this, OK?"

She rested her hand on his arm and squeezed it. "I can tell. Why is it bothering you now?"

He shook his head. "I don't know. It's like my brain is trying to tell me something, make me remember something, but I can't put my finger on it and it's driving me nuts." He smiled. "And not talking to you hasn't really helped any."

Clara squeezed his arm again. "I really am sorry. Emma's the one who pointed out that I should apologize."

"Emma? Ernest's Emma?"

Clara nodded. "I had dinner with her last night. She's so sweet and I think a little lonely. She has children with her second husband, and they have children of their own. I'm just not sure how much time they really have for her."

"So, you made friends with her?" His smile grew wider. Clara could see the old Will coming back to life.

"You know I did. I think I'll make dinner at her place a regular thing. She really seemed to enjoy the company."

"You should ask Harry along sometime. I'm sure he'd love to meet her."

Clara narrowed her eyes. "You think so?"

Will shrugged. "What could it hurt?"

Clara agreed and followed him into the precinct. Alice watched them, her eyes narrowing as they walked to the elevator. Will didn't give her a second glance, not even to smile in her direction. Clara figured he could be only so nice before he gave up. Alice hadn't brought in a peace offering of any kind, at least not that Clara had seen. Clara figured that if Alice was going to ignore her advice, then she could ignore Alice.

Back in Evidence, Will sat at Clara's desk as she paced in front of it. At his own desk, Morgan scribbled notes. "So, Harry is probably the grandkid of old Ernest. Dad's been dead for a bit. Wouldn't have had access to the cage anyway. And Will, you don't think Harry had anything to do with this?"

Will shook his head. "No way. Harry had no need for the knife. He's very close to his grandparents, the adopted ones. He didn't know about Ernest until well after Kelly Jo had died. He said he didn't look into it until someone asked him why he never had before."

Clara stopped pacing. She tapped her foot against the floor. "So we're back to square one. It has nothing to do with Ernest."

Morgan tapped his pencil on the notepad. "Now hang on. The knife is the connection. What we really need to find out is how that kid got it. The one who stabbed me with it."

Clara bit her lip. "And how would we do that?"

Morgan stood. "Leave that to me." He strode out of the room, his limp barely noticeable. Will and Clara exchanged a glance, both looking confused.

When Morgan came back, the captain was with him. Today she was wearing a dark blue pantsuit. Her black heels glistened in the dim light. She folded her arms and leaned against Morgan's desk. "Morgan says you three have some theories I should hear. So, let's hear it."

Clara looked at Morgan, who nodded. "The knife used to kill Kelly Jo … it was used in other cases. It was originally discovered in the leg of a man in a trailer. Collected and logged in as evidence. Then it disappeared. Next, it ended up in Morgan's leg, which led to it again being logged in as evidence. Then it was used to kill Kelly Jo."

The captain nodded. Clara could feel sweat dripping between her shoulder blades.

"We originally believed the connection to be with the original owner," she continued. "But that was a dead end. What we need to find out is how the kid who stabbed Morgan got the knife. That might lead us somewhere."

"To do that, you'd have to talk to him." The captain looked over her shoulder at Morgan. "And by you, I mean you, Morgan." She looked at Clara. "Clara is a civilian. An intern at best. She can watch, but she can't be in the room and she can't ask any questions."

Clara nodded. "Yes, ma'am."

The captain stood, pulling her suit jacket straight. "Good work, you three. Keep at it." She walked out and closed the door behind her.

Will grinned at Clara. "You were amazing."

Clara high-fived him, adrenaline pulsing through her veins. "That was such a rush. I was afraid I was talking too fast."

"You were but she kept up pretty well." Morgan couldn't keep the chuckle from his voice. "Nice job. Now that we have the go-ahead, I can set up the interview. Probably won't be until next week sometime, so until then, we should all get back to our regular duties." He looked at Will, who stood.

"Message received, sir. I'll be downstairs if you need me." He strode out, leaving Clara alone with Morgan and a new box of evidence to be cataloged. In her mind, the weekend couldn't go by fast enough. In reality, she was going to wish it hadn't ever come.

15.

HALLOWEEN PLANS

Clara got home that evening to find Anthony waiting on her doorstep, roses in hand. "I wanted to surprise you with dinner, but I see you beat me to it." He motioned at the Chinese takeout boxes in her hands and smiled as she opened the door for him.

"There's enough for the two of us. Let's share." She set down the boxes and grabbed a vase from her cupboard to put the flowers in. "They're beautiful."

"They made me think of you." He kissed her forehead. The scent of mint and leather enveloped her.

"Mmm, you smell delicious."

He laughed. "Who? Me? Nah, I just smell like a guy." He flexed for emphasis, pulling a giggle out of her.

At the table, Clara filled him in on the case. "We get to talk to the guy next week. Well, Morgan gets to talk to him. I get to watch."

Anthony chewed, his forehead scrunched in thought. "So, you believe Will when he says it's not this kid?"

Clara nodded.

"And you think the bad guy will just tell you where he got the knife from?"

Clara shrugged. "I don't think it'll be that easy, but who knows? He's been locked up for a while. Maybe he'll be willing to talk."

"Speaking of Will…"

Clara's head whipped up.

"Any change between him and Alice?"

"No. She's still being weird and creepy. Even after I talked to her and gave her advice. Something is very off about that chick. I feel bad for even suggesting that he ask her out."

Anthony smiled. "You just want to see everyone happy. It's OK." He paused. "What about Hailey?"

Clara's eyes narrowed. "What about her?"

"For Will."

"For Will what?" Clara could barely get out the words. Her teeth were clenched so hard, her jaw hurt.

"To date? I mean, you never know. They might have something in common."

"Will, have something in common with a sorority girl? I don't think so." Clara jammed some orange chicken into her mouth, chewing louder than needed.

"There's more to her than just the sorority. She's pretty smart once you get to know her."

"Yeah, smart enough to convince all four of those dummies to date her. Even after breaking up with the others." Clara reached for a spring roll and shoved it into her mouth. She refused to look at him. She didn't want to talk about Hailey.

"Are you sure this is about Hailey?"

Clara looked at Anthony, her eyes wide. "And what else would it be about?"

Anthony reached his hand toward her, stopping short of touching her. "Are you sure it isn't about Will?"

Clara's mouth fell open. She snapped it shut, then searched her mind for the right words. "I don't know what you're talking about, Anthony."

"You like Will." The words came out so soft, Clara could almost pretend she hadn't heard them. Almost.

"As a friend." Her hands dropped to her lap. Her right hand covered the ring on her left.

"A friend who you talk about all the time. Who you spend every day with." Clara could hear the question in his voice, even if he wouldn't say it out loud.

"No, Anthony, I don't like Will in that way." She took his waiting hand and squeezed it hard. "I love you. Will is just a friend. If you think he'd like Hailey, I don't see why we couldn't try it. I just don't want him to get mad at me for continually setting him up."

Anthony smiled, the relief plain on his face. "Then invite him to the Halloween party this weekend. He can meet her in a group environment. No pressure if it doesn't work."

Clara groaned and lay her head on the table. "That's this weekend? I totally forgot. What are we going as again?"

"Don't worry, babe, I got this covered. All you gotta do is show up and be your normal, beautiful self."

Clara lifted her head and looked at him through squinted eyes. "Why does that worry me even more?"

The devilish grin he gave her made her stomach drop. She was definitely in for a surprise this weekend.

***

Clara stood in front of the full-length mirror in her bedroom, twisting this way and that. She had to admit, Anthony had done a good job picking out her costume. They were going as a blackjack dealer and a showgirl, wearing red and black to match each other. Anthony wore black slacks, a white button-up shirt, and a red-and-black striped vest with fake cards poking out of a pocket. Clara's outfit didn't leave much to the imagination. With a red corset top, black lace trimming, a black lace tutu skirt, and black webbed pantyhose, she could knock out a room just by stepping into it. Sliding on her black heels, Clara bit her lip and looked at herself one last time. She had piled her hair on top of her head in a messy, curly bun, with ringlets framing her face. "Here goes nothing."

She stepped out of the bedroom and twirled for Anthony's inspection. His face lit up as his eyes took her in. "Wow."

"Is that a good 'wow'?" She gulped and looked at her toes.

He stepped forward and lifted her head by her chin. "It's an 'I-don't-know-what-else-to-say wow.'"

She smiled. "OK. You don't look too bad yourself." She brushed imaginary lint off his shoulder and looked up at him. His hazel eyes seemed to see only her. He bent in to kiss her but was interrupted by a knock at the door. "That must be Will," Clara said. She went to answer it, looking back at Anthony before she pulled open the door.

Will stood in the doorway, speechless. He had settled for going as a space cowboy, figuring it could be dashing in a geeky sort of way. Beige pants, maroon shirt, dark brown trench coat, with empty holsters at his hips. He gave Clara a shaky smile. "What do you think?"

She grinned. "I think you're missing your weapons."

He held up a bag. "I couldn't decide on water guns or a Nerf gun, so I got both." He set the bags on the table

211

and turned to Anthony. "Blackjack dealer. I like it."

Anthony gave him a once-over. "Space cowboy. You'll have all the girls swooning."

Will shrugged. "That's never really been a goal for me." He opened the bags and pulled out the boxes with his fake guns. He handed one box to Clara. They quickly opened them. Clara filled the water gun at the sink, then handed the gun to Will so that he could slide it into his holster. He patted both hips, smiling. "Ready to go. Let's get this party started."

Clara drove, insisting that because she wasn't old enough to drink, her driving made the most sense. In her mind, this also gave her an out if she decided to leave the party early—something she would never admit to Anthony. While she drove, he held her hand and rubbed his thumb over the backs of her fingers. The sensation sent chills up her spine.

When they pulled up to the house, Clara's mouth dropped open. It had been completely transformed. Cobwebs hung from the porch rafters and were strung across the open front door. Jack-o-lanterns had been placed in various spots around the porch and in the front windows, their spooky smiles lighting the way. Orange lights were strung around each window, giving the porch a sickly orange glow.

Anthony climbed out of the car and walked around to Clara's side. He opened the door for her. "My lady." She took his hand and let him pull her out of the car.

The inside had been transformed as well. Bodies were packed closely together, with people barely able to move. Will kept close to Clara, not wanting to get lost in the crowd. Anthony pulled Clara to the living room, where the other guys were gathered around the fireplace. "Is this like a meeting spot or something?" she asked.

Anthony didn't answer. He just smiled at her and stopped in front of them. "Gentlemen."

They nodded at him, their eyes glued to Clara. She felt like a peacock on display, her feathers out for all to see.

Taking in their outfits, Clara realized they all matched. Each one was dressed as a blackjack dealer, though they were wearing different colored vests. They were wearing the same colors that they'd been sporting the first night she'd met them, except for Darren, who wore orange. Jay was in green, Charlie in yellow, and Jaxon in black. Jaxon was shuffling a deck of cards. "So, when are we going to play?"

Clara looked from Anthony to the guys. "Play?"

Anthony nodded. "Yeah, blackjack. The table is set up out back. We could head out there now." The guys nodded, filing out. Clara looked at Will, who shrugged and followed them out.

Clara stopped Anthony before he could go any farther. "Where's Hailey?"

Anthony looked around and narrowed his hazel eyes. "Not sure. Haven't seen her yet. But she'll be here.

She always is." He led Clara out back, where a hazy orange glow covered the pool area. A fog machine pulsed off to the side. A DJ stand had been set up on the back porch, and the music was haunting.

A blackjack table sat at the far end of the pool. In front of it stood a woman dressed as a dealer. When she got closer, Clara realized it was Hailey. Clara looked at Anthony to see if he'd had any idea, but his face remained blank. He looked at Clara, winked, and then threw an arm around Will. "Will, I want you to meet Hailey. Looks like she's our dealer for the evening. She's a very smart cookie and has a fast hand, so keep your eye on her, OK?"

Will nodded and smiled at Hailey. She smiled back, but Clara noticed that her eyes lingered on Anthony, barely giving Will a second glance.

The boys sat at the table while Clara stood behind Anthony. Jay looked up at her. "Wanna get in on this?"

Clara shook her head. "I'm good. I'd rather watch."

"That's what she said." Darren's face turned red at Clara's look. He held up his hands. "It's just a saying."

Clara rolled her eyes and watched as Hailey dealt the first hand. It took Clara a bit to pick up on the game. She could see that Jay was much better at playing than anyone else at the table. Will wasn't bad, able to make small bets and win, but Anthony ended up losing his whole pot in less than five rounds. He grinned up at her, looking sheepish. "I lasted longer than last time."

Clara leaned over and wrapped her arms around his neck as they watched the others play. "You play a lot?"

He nodded. "At least once a week. Not for these high stakes, though. I think they're showing off."

"For who?"

He looked up at her. "You. Or Will. Or both."

Clara shook her head and straightened up. "I'm going to get some punch."

Anthony stood up and took her arm. "I'm coming too." He looked back at the table. "Be back in a bit."

Everyone just nodded, their attention fixed on the game.

In the kitchen, Anthony poured two cups full of punch, then handed one to Clara. "You have something to tell me. I can see it in your eyes. Spill."

Clara grinned. "There's been a development in my case." At his "continue" gesture, she said, "I found the knife. The one used to kill Kelly Jo. It had been used in two other crimes, one an accident, the other not so much. It had been logged in both times but went missing between them. We go this week to talk to the last person to have it, to find out where he got it from."

Anthony whistled. "That really is a development. I bet you're super excited."

"I can't wait. This is going to be amazing. I get to watch an interrogation. Dad would never let me do that."

Anthony set down his cup and pulled Clara close to him. He kissed her forehead, then her cheek, and then her lips, lingering there the longest. "I've missed you. I've missed seeing you like this. Lately, I feel like all we do is argue and not get along. I don't want that for us."

"I don't either. I'm sorry I've been so terrible." Clara looked up into his eyes, getting lost in their depths. "I know I haven't been very accepting of the frat. I just felt really left out and abandoned when you joined. All this time I thought we would get to spend together, you spent with them. But that was unfair of me. I should've been supportive."

Anthony leaned forward and pressed his forehead to hers. "I should've realized how lonely you were. I'm the one who asked you to join me out here. I'm the one who talked you into moving. And then I ditched you because I'm an idiot. Forgive me?"

"Only if you forgive me."

"Deal." They sealed it with a kiss, Anthony pressing her back against the counter. They would've stayed like that for longer if they hadn't been interrupted by someone clearing their throat behind them. Turning, they found Hailey standing with her hands on her hips.

"So this was a set-up, huh?"

Anthony gulped, his grip on Clara tightening. "What?"

Hailey tilted her head. "That guy out there. You brought him for me. You invited me so you could hook me up with someone else, didn't you?"

Anthony started to shake his head, then thought better of it. "Yes. He's a nice guy. I thought you might like him."

Rage flowed from Hailey's crystal-blue eyes. "Like him? Why would I like him when I want you? What about what we shared together?"

Clara took a step forward, her heart sinking into her stomach. "Shared?"

Hailey turned her attention to Clara, almost like she hadn't even realized she was there. "Yeah, shared. He's been pretty bummed out lately, you being too busy for him and all. Cried on my shoulder about how he felt like he was losing you, how he really wanted to keep you, and how he didn't know if that was possible. Fearing, mind you, that you were falling for another guy." She looked over her shoulder. "Kind of a downgrade, if you ask me." She looked back at Clara. "So I comforted him. Held his hand, patted his back, told him it would be all right. Then I kissed him. And do you know that for a good four seconds, he didn't pull away? He didn't react at all, but he didn't pull away."

Anthony's mouth hung open. All the color drained from his face.

Clara stepped back and wrapped her arms around her midsection. "You kissed him?"

Hailey shrugged. "Sure. He's not bad. I bet he's better when he actually puts effort into it."

Clara took another step back and shifted her gaze to Anthony. "And you didn't tell me."

He turned to her, his arms hanging limp at his sides. "I thought it didn't matter, that it wasn't a big deal. If we got Hailey a boyfriend, she'd leave me alone and I'd never have to think about it again. Clara, you have to believe me that it didn't mean anything. As soon as I realized what was happening, I pushed her away. I love you. Only you."

Clara fidgeted with her ring and looked up into his face, truly seeing it for the first time in ages. His hazel eyes were ringed with worry lines. Underneath them were purple bags. This had been bothering him, whether he wanted to admit it or not. "And yet you kept this from me, instead of telling me immediately so that we could work through it together. You didn't trust me."

He grabbed her hands and pulled her against him. "It was never about not trusting you. I was trying to figure out how to say it, how to tell you that I felt like I had betrayed you. I didn't know how to put that into words."

Clara pulled her hands away and held them against her chest. "I don't know how to respond to this. I need time, Anthony. Space. To think, to figure out what I want. To figure out if I can even trust you." She spun on her heel and stomped out of the kitchen, then out of the house entirely. In her car, she shot Will a text, telling him that if he wanted a ride back to her place, she was leaving, NOW.

Within minutes, Will climbed into the passenger seat, looking worried. His brow crinkled as he watched her. She bit her lip to keep the tears at bay, as she refused to cry in front of anyone. They drove home in silence, neither knowing what to say.

As he climbed out of the car at the apartment, Will turned to her and held up a hand. "I know it's none of my business, but I really think he's sorry and he didn't mean it. That doesn't make it right. That doesn't make it fair. But she played on his emotions. She's a manipulator if I ever saw one and they're good at what they do. Just so you understand." He closed the car door and headed down the street. "I'll see you on Monday."

Clara watched him walk away. A tear finally escaped down her cheek. She brushed it away and headed inside, feeling herself break apart as she threw open her apartment door and tossed everything on the table. Bending over, hands on her knees, she let out the scream that she had been holding in. Her tears finally fell as her heart broke in two.

16.

HEALING

Clara spent all of Sunday in bed, not moving. She called her mother to cry, needing to hear her comforting voice over the phone. From her mother's end of the line, Clara could hear bacon cooking on the stove. Rodney and Jasmine were arguing over who was going to get the first piece. Clara smiled through her tears, glad to hear her family. "Hey, Mama."

"Clara, baby, do you have a cold? Are you feeling OK?" In her mind's eye, Clara could see her mom flipping bacon with her favorite spatula, her dark blonde hair pulled back from her thin face.

Clara wiped her nose with the sleeve of her nightshirt. "No, Mama. Anthony and I had a fight. I'm not even sure we're still together." Clara looked at the engagement ring she had placed on her nightstand. She watched it glint in the morning light.

"Tell me what happened."

Clara spilled her guts, talking about the frat and how she felt ignored, left alone most of the time. Then she told her mother about Hailey, a girl who seemed to be on the prowl for any new blood at this particular frat. She told her mom about the Halloween party and how she'd thought that maybe Will could distract Hailey, but that Hailey had a one-track mind. Then she told her about the kiss and how betrayed she felt. When she finished, Clara lay back and closed her eyes, tears coursing down her cheeks.

For a minute, Mrs. Young didn't say anything, letting her daughter process. When she did, her voice came out in a whisper, just loud enough for Clara to hear. "I'm sorry this happened to you, sweetie. Anthony is getting his first taste of freedom after having to be responsible for so long. It hurts to know that you're being hurt during this process." She paused, trying to find the

225

right words to heal her daughter's heart. "This isn't an easy road to follow. You have to decide whether you can trust him again. Only you know that answer. You have to decide whether you want to work through this, figure out if he truly is the one for you."

Clara sighed. "I know, Mom. I just don't know the answer to that yet. I still love him, but I've been so hurt that I don't know where to begin. Or what he would have to do to make me trust him again."

"He won't be able to make you do anything. This isn't something that can just have a Band-Aid slapped over it. He's going to have to earn back that trust and no one knows how long that takes. Every situation is different." She paused and Clara could hear bacon hitting a plate. In the background, Rodney called dibs. "Right now, you need to just take care of yourself. Instead of wallowing, go get your favorite meal, get your nails done, and try to feel better about yourself. This had nothing to do with you and everything to do with him trying to figure out who he is. Now you need to figure out who you'll be without him."

Clara thanked her mother and told her to give her love to her siblings, then hung up. While her mother's advice was good, it didn't propel Clara out of bed. Instead, she ordered takeout and ate it in bed while watching reruns of her favorite shows for the rest of the day. She didn't remember the interrogation until that night, as she was closing her puffy eyes to fall asleep. She hoped she'd feel better in the morning. In her current state of mind, she wasn't looking forward to being around other people.

***

The next morning, Will met her at the precinct, coffee and donuts in hand. "I know it's not much but I hope this helps." Clara smiled as she took a tentative sip, the rich aroma tickling her nose. She reached for a Boston crème and licked some of the chocolate off the top. "Have you talked to him yet?"

Clara shook her head. "I don't think I could handle that right now. I just need some time." She noticed Will's eyes lingering on her empty left hand. "I have to figure out what I want too. And whether what I want matches what he wants."

Will raised an eyebrow. "But don't you have to talk to him to find out what he wants?"

Clara looked up at him. "Maybe I should figure out what I want first. Then see if we're on the same page." Will scratched his chin and stared at her. "What?"

He shrugged. "It just seems to me that you're setting him up for failure. You're going to figure out what you want, alone, then expect him to have figured out the same thing without your ever talking to him about it. Maybe reconsider that idea, OK? That's all I'll say on the matter." They walked past the front desk without a second glance. In the elevator, Will smiled. "Alice's glare doesn't even bother me anymore. It's like

Harry said: If you don't pay attention to it, it stops affecting you."

"Harry said that about Alice?" Clara couldn't keep the curiosity out of her voice.

Will nodded. "Yeah. Apparently, I'm not the first guy she has taken an interest in. He said it took a couple months for her to move on to someone else."

Something about this bugged Clara but she couldn't quite put her finger on it. She pushed the matter to the back of her mind and promised herself that she would explore it in more detail later, when her head was clearer. She pushed open the evidence room door and smiled at Morgan as she walked in. "Will brought donuts." Morgan smiled up at Will and took a glazed one for himself.

Will leaned against Clara's desk. "So, when is the big interrogation?"

Morgan looked at Clara. "Tomorrow morning. We're going to the prison to interrogate him there. We'll meet here and drive over together."

Clara nodded and pulled a file out of the box on which she was working. "Sounds good to me. I can't wait to hear what he has to say."

Morgan looked between the two of them. "You and me both."

17.

INTERROGATION

The next morning, Clara got into Evidence 10 minutes early, as she'd been too excited to sleep any longer. Morgan eyed her as she walked in.

"Morgan, how early do you get here?" she asked.

He shrugged. "Probably about two hours before you."

"And you leave when I do? Why such long hours?"

"Because it's important that I'm here as much as possible. There's a night guy, but I always worry something isn't getting done."

Clara stopped, her purse halfway down her arm. "Wait, there's a night guy? How have I not seen him?"

Morgan shrugged and flipped a page in the newspaper he was reading. "He's supposed to get here before we leave and be here when we come in but he doesn't always make it on time." At Clara's look, he shook his head. "OK, he's never on time. And he always has to leave early. But he's a good kid. So as long as he locks up behind himself, I don't say anything."

Clara dropped her purse. "So, he has a key?"

Morgan gave a small nod. "Yep."

"You told me only two people had keys. That means there's a third and we've never even talked to him. What if someone stole his or something?"

"He would've told me. I really didn't think about it at the time. Again, he's a new measure the captain enacted after Kelly Jo died. He's been here almost two years and I'm still getting used to him."

Clara sat in her chair and looked at Morgan. "Change is hard, isn't it?"

He met her gaze and nodded. "Very much so. You going through some change yourself?"

She nodded and looked down at her empty left hand. "Just trying to figure out what I really want to do. And if I made the right decisions."

Morgan stood up and glanced at his watch. "Time to go. We got to get to Cleveland in the next three hours."

Clara followed him out the door and watched as Harry walked past him into the room. Morgan handed him the keys, smiling. "You know the drill, Carver." Harry saluted and winked at Clara as the door closed on his face.

The drive took a little under two hours, as Cleveland Correctional Center wasn't too far from College Station. Morgan offered to drive and Clara let him, not feeling up to driving herself. Clara spent the ride with her nose in a book, reading about fictional romances to pass the time. Morgan didn't talk. He just turned up the radio, letting the music fill the car.

When they pulled into the parking lot, Clara lifted her head and rubbed her eyes. Morgan turned to her, serious. "You will stay in the viewing room and watch. I won't be able to hear you, so you can't ask any questions. Take notes and write down anything that you find off or interesting, OK?"

Clara patted her purse. "Notepad and pen are ready." She grinned, trying to get a smile out of him, but to no avail. Morgan was in serious cop mode so Clara decided to let it go. She'd get a smile out of him later.

Clara followed Morgan inside, keeping her head down. Everywhere she looked, she saw grey. Grey walls, grey tables, grey chairs. It all blended together in one grey blob. She watched the cop who led them back to a meeting room, noticing his strong arms and broad shoulders. His shirt seemed to be straining against the muscles. The cop showed Morgan into one room, then Clara into the one next to it. "You'll be

able to see and hear him through there."
He pointed at the mirror, then closed the
door as he stepped out. Clara stepped up
to the mirror and took in the room on
the other side.

Again, everything looked grey.
The table had a wooden top, but it was
the only sign of color in the whole room
besides Morgan, who sat at a chair, his
arms crossed. To his right, a door
opened and a handcuffed man shuffled
in, accompanied by another officer. The
man sat in the chair across from Morgan.
For this meeting, Morgan had asked that
he stay cuffed, mainly because he didn't
know how the kid was going to react.
They sat in silence for what seemed like
hours before Morgan finally asked, "How
are you holding up in here?"

The man—more like a kid—just
gave him a disgusted look. His hair had
been shaved close to his head and his
dark eyes seemed sunk into his face. His
skin was tight against his high
cheekbones. One gold tooth gleamed in
the light. In the fluorescent lighting, the

contrast between the two—the kid a pale, almost sickly, yellow and Morgan a dark ebony—was striking. "What do you care?"

Morgan leaned forward, his hands pressed against the edge of the table. "Just trying to be friendly. You've been here, what, almost three years?"

The kid nodded, his eyes on the table. "Yeah. You would know. You put me here."

"You stabbed me. What else was I supposed to do?"

The kid looked up. Something flashed in his eyes. "Cut me some slack. Let me go."

"We did cut you some slack. You didn't get the max punishment. You'll be released soon."

"Then why are you here?"

"I want to know how you got the knife. It's different from any I've seen, and I'm really curious about where you acquired it."

The kid scoffed. "After all this time?"

Morgan spread his hands wide and smiled. "I was stabbed, remember? It took me a bit to recover and really look into the weapon you used."

The kid bent down and scratched his nose with a cuffed hand. "I stole it."

"You stole it?" The disbelief in Morgan's voice was evident to Clara, even through the glass.

The kid shrugged. "Lifted it off some lady. She didn't even see it coming."

Clara could see Morgan tense, his shoulders almost touching his ears. "A lady? Where was this lady?"

"Some bar downtown. I didn't even know she had it on her 'til we started dancing. I took it off her before she even noticed. Then I left, taking the knife with me. I thought something that big would come in handy." He gave

Morgan a pointed look. "Guess I was right."

Morgan stood and shoved back the chair. "Thanks for the info. Good luck." He walked out the door, leaving the kid to sit in the room alone. Clara scribbled madly on her pad, excitement thrumming through her veins. Girl. The killer was a girl. There weren't that many female cops at the precinct. This really shrank the suspect pool quite a bit.

Back in the car, Morgan tapped the steering wheel. "Well, what did you think?"

"Sad kid."

Morgan nodded.

"The killer is a female. A woman broke in twice. Once to steal the knife, the second time probably to steal it again but she ended up having to kill Kelly Jo and leave it."

"Yes. Question is, why?"

Clara looked at Morgan. "Why what?"

"Why steal the knife? What significance does it hold? Why take it at all?"

Clara shrugged. "Maybe she saw it in the first case and really liked it."

Morgan shook his head and started up the car. "No, I don't think so. We're missing a piece of the puzzle. I can feel it."

Clara arched an eyebrow at him. "Cop's gut?"

Morgan just grunted and headed back to College Station.

Clara leaned against the window and looked out at the passing scenery. Morgan was right. Something was off. Why would anyone take the knife unless it meant something to them? And the only person with a connection to the knife was Harry, who definitely wasn't a woman. That left them back at square one. Clara felt like the truth was staring her in the face, but she didn't know how to access it. She closed her eyes, hoping it would become plain soon.

RENEE MARSKI

18.

DINNER WITH EMMA

Harry stopped Clara as she walked past him into Evidence once she and Morgan got back. "Will told me about Emma. I'd love to meet her if that's OK."

Clara looked up into his grey eyes. She was surprised to find a bright yellow ring circling the irises. Emma's eyes, Clara realized. Harry had his grandmother's eyes. "I think she'd like that. Would tomorrow night be OK? It's become our standing date."

Harry nodded, a small smile crossing his lips. "That sounds great. Just get me her address so I can meet you there."

Clara went home ecstatic. Emma was going to be so happy to meet her grandson. It would give her the closure she seemed to need. Clara couldn't wait to do that for her.

At the apartment, she found flowers waiting in front of her door. Lilies, her favorite. The pink in the center of the flowers stood out against the white. She carried them inside while looking for a card. Anthony's easy scrawl caught her eye, making her breath quicken. "I'm ready to talk whenever you are. Take all the time you need. I love you." Clara gulped. She set the flowers on her small table. It was sweet, but it was just another reminder of all the things he was so good at, like persuading her to do things. She climbed into bed, her appetite gone.

Clara's phone lit up—a call coming in. She looked at her screen and was surprised to see that it was from her sister. After talking to her mom, Clara had talked to the girls, but none of them had agreed on what she should do. Hannah had been for a breakup but Stacy and Tracy were adamant that she hear him out, try to work things out. And

Clara just didn't know what she wanted. She answered her phone, pulling a pillow her to chest. "Hey, sis."

Jasmine gasped on the other end. "You actually answered."

"Sorry, it's been a rough week."

"I know. Stacy called me."

Clara ground her teeth in frustration. "Why would she do that?"

"Because you needed me." Coming from Jasmine, it sounded like the most natural thing in the world.

"Jaz, I know that you're super smart and all, but I don't think brains can fix this."

Jasmine laughed. "No they can't, but maybe I can help you figure it out logically. Let's think about this, OK? You didn't like the frat, right?"

"Right." Clara suppressed a groan.

"But he spent most of his time there. Instead of making yourself available, showing up to see him, asking

243

to come over, you pulled away, buried yourself in work, anything you could find."

"Maybe."

Jasmine snorted. "No maybes. We both know that's what you did. Then, he gets vulnerable. Because, to him, it feels like you're pulling away. You guys fight, quite a bit actually, over the frat. Am I right?"

"Yes." Clara groaned into the phone, unable to stifle it this time.

"Stay with me here. You fight. He's frustrated and upset. This girl, who has managed to sink her claws into every guy in that house, sees him like this. She sees her chance to make a move. So she makes it. His response is to reject her, then not tell you. Sucky on his part? Yes. Understandable? Also yes."

Clara sat up, the pillow falling away. "No, Jasmine, not understandable. He kept it from me."

"Clara, what would you have said if he had told you? Who would you have blamed? Him? Or the frat? It would've been one more reason for you to hate the frat. He was trying to get you to accept it, to accept him."

"But why hide it, knowing she'd be at every party, ready to tell me?"

"He didn't expect her to. He thought she'd be embarrassed at his rejection and keep it to herself. But he didn't count on her being vindictive as well as manipulative." Jasmine's words made sense, even if they hurt.

Clara sighed and closed her eyes. "Jaz, why are you so smart?"

"Because I am." Clara could hear her sister's smile on the other end of the line. "Look, talk to him. You love him, Clara. You wanted to marry him. One kiss, a kiss he didn't even want or ask for, shouldn't be the reason you don't get that. Yes, there's a rift between you two but it can be fixed. If ours can be fixed, then yours with Anthony can be."

Clara chuckled. "Ours wasn't a rift. There was just a big, scary boy in the way."

Jasmine laughed. "I guess you could describe it that way."

Clara paused, searching for the right words. "How are you, Jaz? Really? I know I haven't called as much as I should-"

"Clara, I'm fine. I still see my therapist. I still go to group. I'm working through it. I'm so much better than I was and I'll get better every day. Your life doesn't have to halt for mine. I'll get there." She laughed. "I've decided what I want to go to college for."

"What?" Clara held her breath in anticipation.

"Therapy. I want to be a psychologist and help other people the way I've been helped."

Clara squealed and pulled the phone away from her ear, then smashed it back. "That's wonderful, Jaz! You'll be so good at that!"

Jasmine giggled. "I thought you might say that. I just hope you're right."

Clara nodded, though Jasmine couldn't see her. "I know you will be. I feel it in my bones."

"Like Dad's cop gut?"

Clara laughed. "Something like that."

"I love you, Clara."

"Love you too, Jaz. Miss you. Call me next week, OK?"

Jasmine agreed, then clicked off, leaving Clara alone with her thoughts of an upcoming dinner and what she was going to do about Anthony.

***

The following evening, Clara stood outside Emma's house, macaroni salad in hand again, waiting for Harry. She had decided not to tell Emma he was coming for two reasons. First, Clara was worried that he would change his mind and not show up. Second, Clara wanted to surprise Emma, as it seemed like Emma didn't get many surprises in her life. When Harry's blue Cherokee pulled into the drive, Clara let out a sigh of relief. She was glad he'd come.

Harry stepped out and pulled something from the passenger seat. As he walked up the front walk, Clara realized he was holding a pan. "You made something?"

He shrugged, his cheeks turning pink. "I made cornbread. My grandma's recipe. It's usually a big hit."

Clara smiled. "I bet she'll love it. Come on."

She led him up the front steps to the bright yellow door. His eyebrows shot up. "Yellow?"

Clara snorted. "Wait 'til you see the inside." She knocked, holding her breath. Emma answered, a yellow shawl wrapped around her shoulders. She smiled at Clara and reached in for a hug.

"Clara, dear, so lovely to see you." She looked behind Clara to Harry. "And who is this handsome young man?"

Clara straightened and motioned Emma forward. "Emma, I'd like you to meet Harry Carver." She let the last name hang in the air as she watched Emma's face. The woman's grey eyes registered first confusion and then understanding. She reached up a hand and gently touched Harry's cheek. A single tear slid down her own.

"Carver? As in the family that I gave my baby to?"

Clara nodded. "Yes, ma'am, one and the same."

Emma pulled her hand back and blinked. "But he's so young. He's not my baby."

Harry cleared his throat. "No, ma'am, I'm your grandson. My dad was the baby you gave up for adoption. He'd be here himself but he passed away a few years ago."

Emma looked around, realizing they were still on the porch. "Goodness me, how rude. Come in, both of you." She ushered them into the kitchen and took the food from their hands. "Sit, sit." She turned to Harry. "Tell me about him. How did he die?"

Harry scratched the back of his neck. "Heart attack. He loved his burgers and didn't love exercise. Refused to take any blood pressure medication."

Emma's brow wrinkled. "Hmm. Heart problems do run in our family. My own daddy died of a heart attack." She looked at Harry's thin frame. "If you exercise, though, you should be alright." She puttered around the kitchen, preparing plates of food to set in front of them. "I made pot roast tonight. I hope that's OK?"

Clara's mouth watered at the smell in front of her. Savory and cloying all once. "My goodness, Ms. Emma, that smells amazing."

Harry picked up his fork and licked his lips. "I'm always down for a good pot roast."

Emma smiled as she spooned food onto their plates. Then she realized what she was doing and blushed. "I'm so sorry. I know you're both adults. I'm just so used to serving my family. Old habits die hard."

Clara shook her head. "Spoon away, Ms. Emma. I'll eat what you give me."

The old lady laughed, the sound a mix of bells and sandpaper.

All talk ceased during dinner. The only sound was the scraping of utensils on plates and the munching of food. The cornbread disappeared faster than Clara could have imagined. By the time they had finished eating, an hour had passed. Harry offered to help Emma with the dishes, so Clara headed into the living room to give them some time alone. She pulled out her phone and noticed that she had a message. She clicked on it and saw that it was from Anthony. *Call me so we can talk. I never meant to hurt you. Love you.* Clara felt the tears welling in her eyes. Why would he bother her now, on this night? She took a deep breath, trying to banish the tears.

"Is everything all right, dear?" Clara turned to Emma, who was standing in the doorway. "Harry is just finishing up the dishes. You look upset."

Clara sat on the couch and set her phone on the coffee table. "It's my fiancé."

Emma sat next to her and nodded. "I noticed you aren't wearing your ring."

Clara's hand moved to the empty spot. "I haven't taken it off since he gave it to me. I feel so naked without it." She chuckled. "I'm just not sure what I'm going to do."

Emma patted her knee. "Tell me."

Clara launched into the story about the party, leaving out nothing. She didn't know how else to convey her feelings to Emma. "I spent all day

Sunday crying, trying to figure out what I wanted. I still don't know."

"But you do."

Clara looked at Emma. "I do?"

"You want him."

Clara shook her head. Emma held up her hands.

"Listen to me. You still want to be with him. Otherwise, he would already have that ring back in his possession. The reason it's so hard for you to decide is that you can't imagine a future without him."

Clara bit her lip. The tears threatened to fall again. "That's true."

"He made a mistake, yes. He should've told you. If you stay with him, you need to set some ground rules. I think that's where the problem has been the whole time. There were no rules for how he was supposed to act at the fraternity. And you need to be more understanding and open to that side of his life."

253

Clara bowed her head. "You're right. I know you are. It's just so hard."

Emma patted her knee again. "Talk to him, sweetie. He obviously loves you. Let him tell you that."

Clara nodded. "I will." She looked up to see Harry standing in the doorway, his arms crossed. Emma motioned him into the room and pointed to a box by her bookshelf.

"Bring that over here, dear. I have some things I want to show you."

Over the course of the next hour, Emma pulled out Harry's dad's baby book and baby pictures to show Harry things about his father that he had never seen before. "He was over a year old when I gave him up, so all the early stuff was with me, not them. He was so smart. He learned to crawl so fast, and he walked soon after that. I couldn't believe how big he was getting." Harry took it all in, smiling at Emma as she talked about the baby she had let go. Emma seemed to light up with the conversation. Clara had never seen her so happy.

As they left, Emma hugged Clara. "Thank you for this. It's been wonderful to meet him." She patted Clara's back. "Go talk to your young man." She hugged Harry, then gave him her number, telling him to call her any time.

In front of Clara's car, Harry stopped. "Thank you, Clara. That's an experience I'll never forget. She's a pretty special lady."

Clara looked back at the house. "She really is."

She turned to get into her car but he stopped her. "I heard you telling her about your fiancé. I know it's none of my business but you should talk to him. Will said that girl seemed like a huge manipulator and we all know what those kinds of people are like. By not speaking to him, you're doing exactly what she wanted you to do. Why else would she tell you about the kiss the way she did?"

Clara nodded. "Thanks for the advice. See you tomorrow." She drove away, trying to think of what to say to

Anthony. She knew she had to say something. She just wasn't sure what it should be.

When she pulled up to her apartment, she realized she wouldn't have long to figure out. The fancy car he had borrowed sat parked out front. Sighing to herself, Clara walked up to her apartment. She stopped when she saw Jay standing outside her door. "What are you doing here?" she asked.

He held up his hands. "I come in peace. I'm here on behalf of Anthony."

Clara rolled her eyes and unlocked her door. She let him in. "He couldn't come himself?"

Jay shrugged, his shirt stretching with the movement. Until now, Clara hadn't realized how tight his shirts always were. "We told him not to. I offered to go instead and try to talk to you for him."

Clara slammed down her purse on the table. "Because I might hurt him?"

Jay shook his head, his eyes more green than blue that night. "No, because we care about him and it's our fault he's in this mess in the first place."

Clara crossed her arms, waiting for him to go on.

"We all know how Hailey is. We know that she likes to hop from guy to guy at the frat. We thought she'd leave Anthony alone because he was taken. We even had him bring you over to prove to her that you were a real person and that he was off-limits. But that didn't work." Jay started pacing. He threw his arms in the air. "We should've banned her ages ago, after everything she's done to the rest of us, but we just didn't think it would be that big of deal. Besides that, her sorority and our frat work so closely together that we didn't want to ruin those relations. Once she was done with one of us, she never looked back. We didn't realize she'd make a move on Anthony and none of us were there when she did. He didn't even tell us what happened."

Clara sat in one of her kitchen chairs, her whole body deflating. "So no one knew?" Clara had secretly hoped that she could somehow blame the frat for this, put the responsibility where she felt it rightfully belonged.

He shook his head. "We didn't. When she told you, that's when we found out. We kicked her out of the house that night, told her to never come back. Then we tried to talk to him, but, man, he was so broken up about it, he would barely speak. Right now he's leaving his room only to go to classes."

Clara couldn't prevent a small smile from escaping. At least he felt bad too. Then she frowned because it seemed he really did feel bad. "You would have stopped her if you'd known? Or made him tell me?"

Jay nodded. "I swear. We don't play around with that stuff. We've been burned enough times as a group to know it's not fair to anyone in the relationship."

Clara rubbed the back of her neck. She felt a headache coming on. "Guess I need to talk to Anthony."

"He's in the car, if you want me to go get him."

Clara sat up, her eyes wide. "What? I didn't even see him."

"I made him hide so you wouldn't. Didn't want to scare you away." Jay pulled out his phone. "Hey, yeah, she'll talk to you. Come up." He smiled at her. "And here's where I take my leave. You have a lovely night." He walked out the door, patting Anthony on the shoulder as he passed.

Anthony stood in her doorway, his hands hanging at his sides. "Can I come in?"

Clara nodded.

He stepped in, closing the door behind him. "Clara, I'm so sorry. I didn't know she'd kiss me and then when she did, I was so shocked and ashamed, I didn't tell anyone. Not even the guys. I knew that if I told you, you'd blame the frat and claim that it was as evil as you believed it to be."

Clara looked up into his beautiful face. The bags under his eyes didn't diminish that beauty. "Anthony, I have to be able to trust you. I have to trust that you'll tell me everything, no matter how scared you are. Otherwise, this will never work. We can't have a relationship that's not based on trust."

He nodded.

She reached into her pocket and pulled out something, then set it in his open palm. "Here."

When he looked down at his hand, he found her ring resting in it. Tears welled in his eyes.

Clara laid her hand over his. "Keep it for me. I'm not saying no and I'm not saying I don't want to be with you. I'm saying we need to work this out and figure us out before we decide to take that big leap. Maybe we rushed into it too fast. There have been so many changes over the last year and we didn't think this through enough."

Anthony closed his hand around the ring and looked into her eyes. "I'm going to put this back on your finger one day. I promise."

She reached up and touched his face. "I don't doubt it. I think first we need to lay some ground rules. Especially with the frat. If that's OK?"

He nodded and moved to the table. They sat together, their heads bent over a notepad as they wrote out rules they thought would be fair. Things like '*No spending alone time with random girls/guys who aren't friends*' and '*No drinking so much you pass out.*' Anthony assured her that he thought the rules were fair. They decided to have dinner together once a week, either going out to eat or eating at her place or at the frat. It would give them a night for just for the two of them. Clara promised to spend more time at the frat house, to be more involved with that side of his life. After two hours, they sat back, bleary-eyed.

261

"I think this is a good start." Anthony yawned and stretched his arms over his head.

Clara nodded. "I agree. And it's bedtime. Work isn't going to be fun tomorrow."

He smiled at her. "How's the case going?"

Clara looked at her clock and cringed. "How about I tell you all about it over dinner tomorrow night? I'm beat."

He stood and stretched out his hand to her. "Until tomorrow night." He kissed her, then left, leaving her standing in the middle of the room. She looked at the list with a smile.

"It's a start. At least we're getting somewhere." She headed to bed, looking forward to dinner the next night.

19.

ONE LAST CLUE

Clara walked past Alice the next morning, barely acknowledging her presence. She had decided that ignoring the glares would be better than giving them any attention. As she waited for the elevator door to open, she felt a presence against her back. Clara spun around and found Alice standing directly behind her, staring in her face. Clara took a step back and pulled her purse against her chest. "Alice, I didn't even hear you walk up. What can I do for you?"

"Did you meet Harry for dinner last night?"

Clara gulped. "Harry?"

Alice rolled her eyes. "Yes, Harry. You know, Ralph's partner. Skinny, cute, grey eyes. That Harry."

Clara nodded. "I did."

"Why?"

Clara bit her lip, trying to decide on the best course of action. For all she knew, no one at the precinct aside from Morgan, Will, and the captain knew about Harry's dad's adoption. If that was the case, the information wasn't something Clara should be sharing with other people. That was up to Harry.

Straightening her shoulders, Clara gave Alice her fiercest glare. "It's personal." She turned back to the elevator, keeping her back straight.

As the door swung open she heard Alice say, "So you're sleeping with him too?"

Clara almost fell over in shock. She spun, a blush rising to her cheeks. "Sleeping with him too? Who else am I sleeping with?"

Alice shrugged. "Will, for one. We're all pretty sure you are."

Clara stepped toward Alice, ignoring the elevator. "I'll have you know I'm not sleeping with anyone. I don't do that. I have a fiancé. Why would I sleep with anyone here?"

Alice looked at Clara's left hand. "There's no ring anymore. I figured you broke up with him for Will. Or was it for Harry?"

"My ring is being cleaned. How dare you assume something about me that you know nothing about? Did you tell other people?" When Alice refused to look at her, instead taking slow steps back to her desk, Clara knew she was right. "You did. You spread this filth to other people. Alice, why?"

Alice dropped the timid act. Determination and hate filled her eyes. "Because you won't keep your hands off them. You're always talking to Will, always hanging out with him. And now you're having dinner with Harry. You don't even know Harry."

"I know enough about Harry to be friendly with him. And I don't have to answer to you. Stop spreading lies about me, Alice. Mind your own business."

Clara walked into the elevator and jammed the button as hard as she could. As the door closed, Alice continued to glare at her.

Clara couldn't shake her anger as she marched down the hall to the evidence room. She threw open the door, not even flinching as it crashed against the wall. Morgan looked up, one eyebrow raised at her.

"Rough morning?"

"Alice is getting on my last nerve. I swear. I've tried to be nice. I've had her over to my apartment. I've tried to give her advice. Instead, she blames me, claims I'm the reason none of the men like her." Clara threw herself into her chair and crossed her arms. "I can't even have one meal with someone without her breathing down my neck."

Morgan leaned toward Clara, his full attention on her. "What did you say?"

Clara shrugged. "I can't have dinner with someone without her breathing down my neck?" He nodded. "Well, yeah, it's just that. She accosted me today because I met Harry last night at Emma's house to introduce them to each other."

Morgan nodded. "The grandmother."

"Yes, the grandmother. Thing is, how did she know?" Clara bit her lip. "Harry must've told her. There's no other way she would've found out. She seemed a little possessive of him."

"I thought she liked Will."

Clara threw her hands up. "I have no idea anymore. But according to her, I'm sleeping with everyone." Clara dropped her head onto her desk. "I give up."

Morgan stood and walked back to the cage. He brought her a box and set it down next to her head. "Focus on work. Let the other stuff go for now. It'll help."

"If you say so." Clara pulled out the first file and spread the papers out before her as the computer booted up. She hadn't been looking at them for longer than five minutes when she called him over. "Morgan, come look at this."

He stepped up behind her, reading over her shoulder. "What's that?"

"It looks like time logs. Like, old-school style, what they used in the military to record the day's events. Does the handwriting look familiar?"

He took one of the pages from her and held it close to his face, scanning the page. "It could be the prior officer's handwriting. It's been a while since I've seen it, so I'm not 100% sure that's what it is."

"But I thought he was losing his memory."

Morgan pulled a second file out of the box and discovered more of the same as the first. "Maybe he was. If so, he must've written everything down. All the comings and goings of everyone who came through that door. That way, if he was ever asked, he could say for sure what had happened, with or without the cameras."

They locked eyes. Clara was barely breathing. "Do you think the logs about the knife would be in here? It went missing sometime between Ernest dying and you getting stabbed. How long of a period was that?"

Morgan looked up at the ceiling, doing the math in his head. "A month, tops."

Clara looked at the box. "Do you think it's in here?"

Morgan pulled out another file. "Only one way to find out."

***

Hours later, they hadn't found anything. The only break they had taken had been for lunch. Clara had met Will at the taco truck and had gulped down her three tacos.

"Busy morning?" Will asked.

Clara nodded. "We found something."

Will looked around, then leaned in closer. "What did you find?"

"Logs. The guy who ran Evidence before Morgan knew that he was losing his memory, so he took meticulous logs. He wrote down everything, every person who came through that door, what they wanted, even when he took his breaks. I think the person who took the knife will be in those logs." Clara paused and took a sip of soda. "Also, did you tell Alice about Harry coming to Emma's with me last night?"

Will's eyebrows shot up. "No. Why would I tell Alice anything? I don't talk to her anymore."

Clara shrugged. "She accosted me when I came in this morning. Ranting about how I'm taking all the single men in the precinct. She pointed out that my ring is gone. Something's not right with her."

Will squared his shoulders. "I'll go talk to her if you'd like."

Clara shook her head. "No, I handled it. I just don't understand how she knew. Is she close to Harry or something?"

Will shrugged. "I mean, he actually dated her for a bit. Remember, I said I wasn't the first person she was interested in. That was Harry. But after her partner died, it kind of fizzled out. He never said why. I don't even know if he still talks to her. I could ask him."

Clara shook her head again. "Nah, it's not a big deal. Just a little creepy is all. It'll be fine. I told her to back off. Hopefully she listens." She grinned. "I've got a dinner date tonight with Anthony. Wish me luck!"

"Well, if she gives you any more trouble, let me know." Will puffed out his chest and gave Clara a big smile. "And good luck!"

Clara stood, smiling back. She patted Will on the shoulder and headed back inside, her mind already back in Evidence with the boxes they had found.

The man had taken meticulous notes, indicating each person who came through the door, what they had brought, what they had checked out, what they had brought back, what he had eaten for lunch, when he had gone to lunch, and for how long he'd been at lunch. He wrote down everything he could think of, the fear of forgetting evident with each word. "He really cared about this job."

Morgan looked up at her. "Once a cop, always a cop."

Clara nodded, hearing her father in those words.

She and Morgan had taken all the files and spread them out on the floor in front of the two desks. People had been stepping around them all day, with Morgan leaving the floor only to help them when they needed it. Still, they hadn't found the dates they were looking for.

"There must be more of these boxes, with more files of these logs." Clara looked at the boxes in front of her. "These are all too early. From a year before the stabbings."

Morgan looked at his, too. "These as well. But now we know there's a pattern. We'll box these back up and look for the next ones." They gathered up the papers and stuffed them back into the box. Morgan went back into the cage for another box just as Clara's phone pinged. She looked at it to see that Anthony had sent her a message. *'Dinner still at 7?'* She looked at her watch.

"Well, crap. Morgan, I'm going to have to take a box to go. I'll look it over tonight after my dinner with Anthony."

Morgan brought out a box and set it on her desk. "This one is lighter. It's probably the most recent one he did, before I took over and he retired. It's probably in there. Text me if you find it." Clara hoisted up the box and nodded as she left the room.

She exited the elevator, barely able to see around the box. Clara passed the front desk, not even stopping to say anything to Alice. As she reached the door, she heard a voice cry out, "Let me get that for you." The next thing she knew, Alice was standing at the door, holding it open. "Taking work home with you?"

Clara nodded. "Just some light reading. Old logs that the previous officer had kept when he ran the evidence room. Not evidence itself, so I can go through it at home."

Alice nodded, eyeing the box. "I can help you to your car if you'd like."

Clara paused, the offer throwing her off balance. "That's very nice of you, Alice, but I'm good, I promise. I got this. See you tomorrow." Clara made it to her car in one piece, then put the box in the trunk before climbing in the front and heading off to her apartment. She had an hour before she met Anthony and she wanted to freshen up a bit before she got there.

She carried the box up to her apartment and set it on the table as soon as she got through the door. Clara went into her bathroom and pulled out her toothbrush and mouthwash. With the water running and her music playing in the background, she didn't hear the door open and close. She shut off the water, spat out toothpaste, and reached for the mouthwash. The minty-fresh tingle always felt rejuvenating. When she glanced in the mirror, the bottle halfway to her lips, her eyes locked on another set of eyes in the mirror. "How did you-" she got out before the world went black.

20.

MISSING DINNER

Anthony sat at the table, alone, playing with the ring on a chain around his neck. When Clara had handed it back to him the night before, he had been devastated. A piece of his heart had broken. But when he had told Jay about it in the car, Jay had reminded him that she hadn't outright rejected him and that they had created a plan to work on their relationship together. Clara had also asked him only to hang on to the ring for her, not to keep it forever. Anthony had to keep reminding himself about this as he sat waiting for her.

After an hour, he was staring at an empty water glass for the third time. He checked his phone again, making sure he still had a signal. He had already tried to call her three times, with no answer. Anthony felt his face start to heat up. She had never stood him up before, but maybe their relationship was more damaged than he thought. Or she was stuck at work and had forgotten. He dialed the precinct, hoping someone would know how to find her. The officer who answered informed him that she had left well over an hour ago but that he could check to see if anyone knew where she was.

Anthony waited for what felt like hours until he heard a familiar voice on the other end of the line. "Anthony?"

Anthony cleared his throat. "Will, is that you?"

"Yes, it is. The desk officer says you're looking for Clara?"

Anthony fidgeted with the tablecloth. "Yeah. She was supposed to meet me for dinner over an hour ago. I tried her cell but got no response, so I figured maybe she got distracted there and forgot about our dinner."

Will snorted. "She definitely didn't forget about your dinner. I promise."

Anthony leaned forward, pressing the phone to his ear. "But she's an hour late, man. Maybe she changed her mind and just hasn't decided to tell me yet."

"Does that sound like something Clara would do?"

Anthony paused. "No, it doesn't." He sighed. "Then where is she?"

He could hear papers rustling on the other end of the line. "She and Morgan made a pretty big discovery today up in Evidence. It might lead to a break in the case. Maybe she got home, got to looking through everything, and lost track of time?"

Anthony rubbed his eyes. "It's a possibility. But she's not answering her phone, which isn't like her. I don't know, man. I've got a bad feeling about this."

More papers rustled. Then a sigh. "Let me check with Morgan. Maybe he's found something. Give me a minute." Will placed Anthony on hold, then dialed Morgan's number. He thought Anthony was just being a paranoid boyfriend but decided it wouldn't hurt to check.

Morgan picked up on the second ring. "Hello?"

"Morgan, hey, its Will. Got a question. This is going to sound weird but you're pretty sure Clara went straight home when she left here today, right?"

There was a pause, then, "Yes, that was her plan. She took a box of those logs home with her. But I don't think she has the right ones. It seems I took the right box home." There was some shuffling, then silence.

Will cleared his throat. "OK. She's late for a date with her boyfriend and he called the precinct looking for her. Just wanted to make sure she hadn't changed any plans." When Morgan didn't respond, Will cleared his throat. "Morgan?"

"Will, what time did Alice leave today?" Morgan's voice sounded tense, something that Will wasn't used to hearing.

Will snorted. "Um, I don't know. The same time she normally does. Why?"

279

"She's the one. She did it."

Will tapped the phone with his pen. "Uh, Morgan, did what? What are you talking about?"

"She took the knife. The old man wrote it down here in his logs. He must've forgotten to put it in the official log. That, or Alice made it disappear, but it's here, when she came in and what she asked to check out. She took the knife, Will."

Will sat back in his chair, the sounds from the squad room fading behind him. "She did what?" On the last word, his voice went up an octave.

"Alice took the knife. Must've lost it at the club. Then realized that it would be recognized when it got checked back into Evidence and tried to retrieve it."

Will sucked in a breath. "Her partner." He slammed his hand down on his desk. "Morgan, her partner died right after your stabbing. He knew. He knew that the knife had been in Evidence before. She let him die to keep it a secret."

"Where does she live, Will?" The calm in Morgan's voice chilled Will.

"No idea but I'm not even sure that's where she's at. Was she gone when you left the building this evening?"

"Yes. That's why I asked when she had left."

Will exhaled, trying to remain calm. "I bet she saw Clara leave. And I bet she knew something was up with the box Clara had. Morgan, she knows where Clara lives. What if she's over there right now?" Will stood up, still gripping the phone.

"Then we go get her. Let the captain know. We're going to keep this low-key, so don't tell anyone else unless the captain says so."

"Roger. One question. Why did she take the knife in the first place?"

"I plan on asking her that when we get her in cuffs." Morgan hung up, leaving Will listening to a dial tone. He looked down at the phone and realized that Anthony was still on hold. After clicking back over, he cleared his throat, trying to remain calm.

"So, look. I just talked to Morgan. We're going to go check on Clara. It's probably nothing, but we'd rather be safe than sorry. I'll have her call you once we get there."

Anthony narrowed his eyes and looked at his refilled water glass. "You're lying. I lived with a liar for most of my life. I can hear it in your voice. What aren't you telling me?"

Will bit the inside of his cheek. "OK, look, I'm going to be straight with you. Morgan knows who took the knife, which is probably the same person who killed our last intern. And she knows where Clara lives. We're heading over there now to check on Clara. She's probably fine."

Anthony shook his head, forgetting that Will couldn't see him. "No way. There's no way she'd go this long without calling me to let me know she was running late. I'm coming too."Anthony paused, Will's words sinking in. "She?"

Will ignored Anthony's question, focusing instead on his previous words. "Whoa, dude. Look, I get that this is your girl, but this is police business. Stay back and let us do our jobs."

Anthony grit his teeth, his empty hand clenched under the table. "I'm going to be there whether you give me the OK or not. I'll stay back but I'm not staying away."

Will whistled. "Fine. But stay back where I tell you. Got it?"

Anthony agreed and hung up. He left a tip on the table even though he'd had only water all evening. Wasn't the waiter's fault he didn't order any food. He rushed out the door and headed to the car. He had to get to Clara's apartment as fast as he could.

Meanwhile, Will headed into the captain's office, relieved to find her still at her desk. "Late night, Cap?"

She looked up, a scowl on her face. "I've told you before-"

He closed the door, cutting off her words. "I know, but I don't really have time for formalities right now. Clara's in danger."

The captain sat up a little straighter and nodded for him to continue.

"Alice took the knife. Morgan and Clara found logs kept by the last guy who ran Evidence. He kept meticulous logs because he was forgetting everything. They each took a box home. Morgan has the right logs, the ones with the proof in them."

"What proof?" The captain looked skeptical.

"Alice checked out the knife and never brought it back. Alice saw Clara leave with the box." Will paused and took a deep breath. "Clara missed a date with her boyfriend this evening. I know for a fact that she was looking forward to it. No call, no text, just didn't show. That's not like her. Alice knows where she lives, Cap. We need to go check on her." Will leaned forward. "Morgan is already on his way. I don't need a big group. Let me just take a couple guys and scope out the situation."

The captain didn't take long to think about it. "Do it. But call me if you need more backup. I don't want another dead intern on my hands. " Will turned to the door to leave but she stopped him. "And Will?"

"Yes, Cap?"

"I want Alice alive. I want to know why she did this."

Will nodded and promised to do his best as he backed out of her office. On his way out, he stopped by Ralph's and Harry's desks.

"Hey, guys. Leaving?"

Ralph stretched, his shirt buttons protesting. "Trying to. Drowning in paperwork as usual."

Will nodded in understanding, then crouched down next to them, keeping his voice low. "OK, look, I need some help. I think Clara's in trouble."

The two exchanged a glance. Will plowed on.

"She and Morgan made a discovery that led Morgan to figure out who killed Kelly Jo. We think that person knew they were about to be caught and went to Clara's to stop her. They thought that the logs Clara had would incriminate them but they didn't realize that Morgan—and not Clara—had the correct logs. Clara's not answering her phone. I need you guys to go with me to check on her. OK?"

They both nodded without hesitation and stood up to follow him out.

In the squad car, Harry asked, "So, who did it?"

Will whipped the car around a corner, lights flashing. "Alice." He gripped the steering wheel, keeping the car steady. "We just don't know why."

A heavy silence hung in the air. Will looked at Harry in the review mirror. Harry looked back, his eyes wide. "I didn't know."

Will narrowed his eyes. "What do you mean you didn't know? What didn't you know?"

Harry kept silent, causing Will to glance over at Ralph. Ralph shook his head, sweat beading on his brow. "Tell him, kid."

Harry wet his lips. "Alice and I dated, right? Before her partner died. About a week before Morgan's stabbing, she told me she had a gift for me, invited me out to some club. I'm not a big club-goer, but when your girlfriend invites you somewhere to give you a gift, you go. Except when I got there, she was distraught. Going on and on about how something was stolen, my gift she said, and how she could never replace it. I tried to comfort her, but she just lost it. Then Morgan was stabbed and rumors started spreading that it was a knife similar to the one we had in evidence. I

287

had wanted to go see for myself, but then Alice's partner died and I forgot. She was different after his death. I couldn't get through to her anymore. She shut me out. I broke up with her shortly after that."

He paused and took a deep breath.

"Thing is, she's the one who encouraged me to find out about my dad's birth family. She helped me look, recommended that I do one of those DNA test things. At one point, she even said she had a lead but she never explained. Then we broke up."

"She took the knife to the club to give it to you, but it was stolen off her before you got there." Will's voice had taken on an edge.

Harry nodded. "That sounds like what happened. So she, what? Went back to Evidence to try to get the knife out again?"

Will nodded. "Except this time, Kelly Jo was in there and went to check on her. Alice stabbed her, stashed the knife, and hoped no one would find it."

"Until Clara did." Ralph looked over at Will. "And she knows where Clara lives because of the double date."

Will slammed on the brakes in front of Clara's apartment building and turned to the two men. "Yes, I brought Alice here. But how was I supposed to know?"

Ralph laid a hand on Will's shoulder. "Not your fault, son. Let's make this right. Let's stop her before she does anything else, OK?"

Will nodded.

Ralph pulled out his sidearm and looked back at Harry. "We go in slow. We don't want to spook her. Which one of you boys do you think she fancies the most?"

Will and Harry exchanged a look. "It's probably me." Will bowed his head.

Ralph nodded. "Then you do the talking. Get her to give you that gun. Tell her we don't want to shoot her but we will."

289

"You want me to bluff?" Will's eye widened in worry.

Ralph smiled. "As best as you can."

They got out of the car and headed into the building. Before they'd reached Clara's street, Will had shut off the lights, not wanting to alert Alice to their presence. As they ran up the steps, Anthony stepped out of the doorway, his arms crossed. Will grabbed him by his shirt and hauled him back from the building.

"Get into the squad car."

"Why?" Anthony tried to push past Will, but Will held a hand against his chest.

"You don't have a gun, you aren't a trained police officer, and you could make the situation worse. Just stay there, OK? If you hear shots, call it in on your cell. Or, better yet, use the radio. Ask for the captain." Will gave Anthony one last shove, then went back to the building, following the other two inside. Anthony huddled in the car and looked up at

Clara's window, praying that they knew what they were doing.

21.

THE TRUTH WILL SET YOU FREE

Clara blinked several times. Her eyes felt like they were glued shut. The back of her head was throbbing. She tried to move only to discover that her hands were tied behind her, wrapped around the back of one of her kitchen chairs. Her feet had been tied to the legs of the chair. She lifted her head, blinking away her confusion, and took in the room. Running water told her she wasn't alone. She was in her apartment, where she had been getting ready for her dinner with Anthony when she had been hit from behind. And not by a stranger. "Alice?"

Alice stood at her kitchen sink, rinsing out a glass. She had taken off her uniform top and draped it over another kitchen chair. Her holster was still strapped to her waist and her hair was still in its neat bun. She turned at the sound of Clara's voice, a smile plastered on her face. "Well, look who finally decided to wake up."

"Alice, what are you doing?" Clara looked at the table, where the box of logs sat.

"I'm here to stop you." She set down the glass and stepped toward Clara.

"Stop me? Stop me from doing what?" Clara tried to keep the fear out of her voice, but by the look on Alice's face, she had failed.

Alice rolled her eyes. "Stop you from finding out the truth." She paused, her smile back. "Well, OK, you've already found out the truth. I'm stopping you from telling other people."

Clara shook her head. "Telling other people what?"

Alice threw her hands up. "Stop acting dumb. You and I both know you're much smarter than that." She pointed at the box. "The logs say it, don't they? They list who came in and what they checked out, don't they?"

Clara nodded, still not following Alice's train of thought. The pain in her head was making it hard for her to focus. "Yes. But what does that have to do with you?"

Alice blew out a breath. "I must've hit you harder than I thought." She put her hands on her hips. "He wrote down when I checked out the knife, didn't he?"

Clara's mouth fell open. "You? You took it?" Alice nodded. "Why?"

Alice grabbed one of the other chairs and pulled it up in front of Clara. She straddled it backward. "I was dating Harry at the time. Really liked the guy. He told me about his dad being adopted and I thought he should find his biological family. We started doing some digging and I managed to find Ernest. Of course, by that time the old man had stabbed himself. But there was the knife, it was right there in Evidence. I knew if I took it, no one would notice. I could give it to Harry as a nice surprise, a connection to his grandfather."

"But you lost it." Even with a concussion, Clara could see where this was going. She looked at the clock over her kitchen sink and realized that she had been out for over an hour. Anthony would come looking for her. She had to keep Alice talking.

Alice nodded again. "Yeah, some punk lifted it off me. Then it got used to stab Morgan and I couldn't just leave it there. Enough people would look at it and realize that it was the same knife. If Ralph saw it, he would know instantly. It was such a unique knife, I didn't have a choice. I had to get it back."

"But Kelly Jo was there."

Alice snorted. "Stupid kid. Couldn't leave well enough alone. She came looking for me, asking if I had found the box and if I needed any help, right as I was slipping the knife into my shirt. I didn't have a choice. I had to stab her." Clara heard no remorse in Alice's voice at all. Alice didn't feel sorry that she had taken a life. "Then my partner-" Alice halted, her voice catching. Clara actually saw tears in her eyes.

Clara's eyes widened. "You let him die."

Alice didn't move.

"That story you told, about how you couldn't get help, how you froze and made the wrong decisions. You could, but he suspected what you had done. He suspected it was you."

Alice leaned in closer, her breath blowing in Clara's face, warm and sweet-smelling. "He told me he was going to take his suspicions to the captain. That he wanted to give me a chance to explain myself. We were there the night Morgan was stabbed. We both saw the knife. He knew instantly what it was. I couldn't get exposed like that."

"But you worked in Evidence with Morgan. Why not take it then?"

"By then, Kelly Jo had died. The security system had been upgraded and

Morgan never left anyone alone in that room. I never had a chance to take it from its hiding place. Then he moved me out."

Clara shook her head. "The captain moved you out. Morgan wouldn't have that kind of power."

"But he has pull with the captain. She listens to him. He's the reason I was moved." Alice stood up and pulled out her gun. She pointed it at Clara. "I really didn't want to do this but it can't be helped. Kills two birds with one stone, though. Now I'll have another shot at Will with you gone."

Clara looked at the gun, then the boxes. "But, Alice, did you even look in the box yet? What if I don't have the right papers?"

The gun dipped, Alice's resolve wavering. "What?"

"Morgan took home a box, too. There were a lot of logs. The man wrote down everything. What if my box is the wrong box and Morgan has the right one? Are you going to kill him, too?"

The gun dropped farther. "Morgan might have it?" The doubt in her voice gave Clara hope.

"Yes. Look, I'm not the only one with a box. Alice, turn yourself in. This has gotten way bigger than you can handle. You're in over your head. Turn yourself in and they may go easy on you."

Alice smirked. "Easy? I killed a cop. There will be no going easy on me." The gun came back up. "Guess I'll have to go to Morgan's after I finish here. Oh well. He was never very nice to me anyway."

Clara squeezed her eyes closed, waiting for the blast that would end her life. Instead, a knock sounded at her door. Alice's head whipped toward the door, then back at Clara. "Are you expecting someone?" Clara shook her head, too afraid to speak. She bit her lip, praying it was Anthony.

Instead, Will's voice sounded through the door. "Alice? Alice, are you in there?"

Alice took a step toward the door, her gun pointed down. "Will? What are you doing here?"

Will sighed. "Alice, I need you to come out here. With your gun holstered."

"Will, why are you here?" Alice's voice shook. Clara could see Alice cracking right in front of her eyes.

There was a pause, and then Will spoke again. "Alice, we know everything. Me, Harry, Ralph, Morgan, the captain. We know what you did. Killing Clara won't protect you. Let her go."

"You came for her." The shakiness left Alice's voice, to be replaced by rage. "That's why you're here. You came for her." Clara watched as the gun shook in Alice's hand.

The handle turned and the door inched open. "Alice, I came for you. I'm here to take you in safely. I'm here to protect you." Will swung the door open wider, revealing him, Ralph, Harry, and Morgan, who had shown up right before Will had knocked on the door. Will held out his hand. "Give me your gun, Alice. We can walk out of here right now, no problem." Will refused to look at Clara, refused to bring Alice's attention back to her. Clara bowed her head, watching them through the curtain of her hair.

"Liar. I'm dead. I killed a cop. The minute I get locked up, I'm dead and you know it."

Morgan pushed to the front, his hands raised. "No, Alice, it's not like that. That was a mistake. You didn't mean for it to happen. He was your partner. Of course it was an accident."

Clara saw real tears in Alice's eyes. "That's right," Alice said. "I didn't mean for him to die. I tried to save him, I swear." Even from her vantage point, Clara could hear the lie.

Morgan did a good job of not flinching. "We believe you. You're one of us. But, Alice, you have to come with us, to the precinct. We have to hear your side of the story." Alice nodded and took another step toward them, her gun outstretched. Will lunged for it and pulled it from her hand as Harry moved for her arm. Seeing her mistake, Alice jumped back and pulled her arms against her chest. Harry fell forward. Alice ran to the window and threw it open.

She turned to them, the cool night breeze ruffling the wisps of hair in her bun. "You don't believe me. This is a trick. You all think I'm guilty. And you're right. I am." She locked eyes with Harry. "I did it for you. I thought we were in love. I just wanted to get you a gift. I thought it would mean a lot to you, something from your grandfather." She looked at Morgan. "But then it was stolen and used against you. Of all the people in that precinct, you had to be the one to get stabbed with it. I had to get it out of there." She looked to Will, her eyes softening. "Kelly Jo caught me and I had to silence her. She didn't suffer, I know that much. I just couldn't be found out. I thought if no one found it, I would be safe. Then we would have a chance."

Alice turned to Clara, her eyes hardening.

"Then you came along and ruined everything. I hope you're happy." She lunged out the window headfirst, her feet together like she was diving into a pool. Will, seeing what she was going to do, lunged after her. He grabbed one ankle as she dove out the window. Clara heard Alice's body whack against the wall outside and watched as Will tried to get a grip on something that would keep him from going out the window after her.

"Not gonna happen, sister. You aren't getting out of it that easily." Her weight almost pulled Will out the window. The only thing keeping Will in place was the fact that Ralph had grabbed his shirt from behind. Will looked back, his lips quivering. "Thanks."

Together, they pulled Alice back in through the window. Clara looked up as Anthony charged into the room, almost knocking Harry to the ground again. Ralph cuffed Alice, who had a cut above her eye and blood streaming down her face. Scratches on her cheek showed that she had hit the side of the building pretty hard. Ralph and Harry escorted her down to the squad car while Morgan and Will stayed behind to secure the crime scene and call the captain.

Anthony untied Clara's hands and feet, then cupped her face in his hands. "I was so worried about you. Are you OK? Did she hurt you?" Clara shook her head. He kissed her forehead. "You really like to get into danger, don't you?"

Clara smiled. "It finds me, not the other way around. But we caught her, Anthony. Kelly Jo gets to rest in peace, knowing her killer was caught." Tears streamed down Clara's cheeks as he pulled her close.

"I know, baby, but do you always have to get this close to death? You're going to make me grey before my time."

She kissed him, his stubble rubbing against her face. "I was raised in this, Anthony. I grew up around it. It's in my blood. I can't just ignore my talents. I can't ignore who I am any more than you can." She closed her eyes. "You're going to make a wonderful veterinarian one day. You have the mind for it. I would never stop you from doing something you were meant to do."

He kissed her forehead. "I know. I just had to ask. You know I support you."

Clara stood up, rubbing her wrists. She looked at Will. "I'm not going to be able to sleep here tonight, am I?"

Anthony looked at her in confusion. "You want to sleep here? After tonight?"

Clara shrugged. "It'll make for an interesting story to tell, don't you think? Something to bring up at the next frat party." She smiled up at him and his eyes lit up.

"Yeah, I guess it would. You can stay at the house tonight. The couch pulls out. I'll text Jay to get it ready for you." He stepped outside to send his message while Morgan and Will took Clara's statement.

"I can't believe she came after me." Clara rubbed her wrists and winced at how raw they felt from the ropes.

Will looked at her wrists. The angry red rings around them made his jaw clench. "She was cornered. She knew it would be only a matter of time before you found out the truth."

Clara looked at Morgan. "How did she not know about those logs?"

"No one did. Until we found them, everyone assumed they were evidence. My best guess? He intended to take them with him, then boxed them up, forgot they were his logs, and stuck them in the cage, not realizing what he was doing. And since they were already there when I took over, I figured we'd find out what was in them when we started cataloging."

Clara rubbed the back of her head, wincing. "Do you think she was the one deleting the files that we were typing in?"

He shook his head. "No, but I'll find out who it was. She must've had help for that part." Morgan walked them to Anthony's car and held the door open for Clara as she climbed in. He handed Clara a bag of peas from her freezer. "Ice that head." He looked at Anthony. "Better keep an eye on her tonight in case she has a concussion."

Clara glared up at him. "I'm fine, Morgan. Right as rain. I'll see you tomorrow."

He nodded and closed the door.

Anthony started up the car and turned to her. "I love you."

She smiled at him. "Love you too." She closed her eyes and fell asleep as he drove.

EPILOGUE.

TIME MARCHES ON

Two Months Later

Clara closed the lid on the last box and brushed the dust off the top. Once there had been no more clues to find, no more murderer to chase down, finishing the cataloging had been smooth sailing. She had managed to do it in less time than she thought. She looked over at Morgan and smiled. "That's the last one. Everything has been digitized. No more paper files."

Morgan carried the box back into the cage and then stepped out, locking it behind him. He stood behind Clara and looked at her computer screen. "It's been a lot easier to do now that the files aren't getting deleted. The more stuff we added, the longer it took to upload every day."

"I still can't believe she convinced the night-shift guy to delete the files for her. And all she had to do was pay him."

Morgan shrugged. "I believe it. He was desperate for money. Falling behind on bills, living beyond his means. She offered him the money he needed, so he did what she asked. What he didn't count on was me noticing or figuring out a way around what he was doing."

Clara looked at her empty desk. "I can't believe it's over. Christmas is right around the corner, and then school starts. It's going to be so different when I get back."

Morgan placed a hand on her shoulder. "You'll do just fine. And when you finish, if you decide you still want to be a cop, I'm pretty sure the captain will hire you."

Clara smiled up at him. "Well, I guess this is goodbye. For now, anyway." She stood and gave him a quick hug, surprising herself.

He returned the hug, which surprised her even further. "Don't be a stranger."

Clara slipped out of his embrace and waved as she headed to the door. She opened it, still looking over her shoulder, only to run into something solid. Looking up, she realized she had run right into Will.

"Going somewhere?"

Clara nodded. "Home. We finished. Last box is done."

Will took her arm and looked over her shoulder. "Well, I need you for one more thing. Captain has a special request."

Clara followed him down the hall, clutching her purse. "Special request? For what?"

He looked over his shoulder. "You'll see."

In the elevator, he hit the button to take them down to the squad room.

As the doors slid open, a chorus rang out, yelling, "Surprise!"

Clara's mouth fell open. Streamers were hanging from the ceiling fans, while balloons were attached to the cubicles. Several people were blowing noisemakers. Will pulled Clara into the room. Someone offered her a cupcake as she walked by.

"Will, what is this?"

"Everyone knew it was your last day. We just wanted you to know how much we'll miss you." The elevator pinged again and Morgan stepped out.

Clara spun on him. "You knew too?"

He grinned.

Clara rolled her eyes. "It's not like I'm not coming back. I have school in the spring right here in town. I'll still be here."

Will held out a plate of tacos, fresh from the truck. "But you won't be here with us. We'll miss you." She took a bite of taco to avoid answering the question in his eyes.

Clara spent about an hour mingling, shaking hands, and eating food. Finally, she knew she had to leave. After another round of hugs, she took the elevator down to the ground floor and stepped out one last time. Anthony had sent her a text, letting her know that he would pick her up for their flight home that night. Her whole family was so excited to see her. For all she knew, they were planning a party, too. The girls had already claimed her for a shopping day next week. And she had set aside some time for just her and Jasmine. Clara felt like the whole vacation had already been planned and she hadn't even gotten there yet.

After stepping outside, she looked back at the building towering over her. Her heart broke just a little to know that she wouldn't be coming back there in the spring. At the same time, she looked forward to the next chapter. Deep down, she knew she would be back there

someday. She could feel it in her gut—
her very young and developing cop gut.

About the Author

Renee Marski is an American writer currently living in Virginia with her husband, daughter, and dogs. She grew up on Sci-Fi, Luke Skywalker being her first love. She currently has several books in the works. Find her on IG

RENEE MARSKI

instagram.com/reneemarskiauthor   or
twitter at twitter.com/reneemarskiaut1

Made in the USA
Columbia, SC
19 September 2022

67582251R00193